SWEET SALT

Other Books by Robert Mayer

THE GRACE OF SHORTSTOPS
MIDGE & DECKER
THE EXECUTION
THE SEARCH

SWEET SALT

ROBERT MAYER

SPEAKING VOLUMES, LLC

NAPLES, FLORIDA

2011

SWEET SALT

ISBN 978-1-61232-052-6

Library of Congress Control Number: 2011921548

To La Donna

In the steam dancing above the mutton stew an eagle barked, and pecked with its shimmering beak at Nina's moon belly, breaking something deep inside and trickling warm liquid down the inners of her thighs. She hurried to the hogan but the false bird followed, spreading pale shadow wings till Nina could scarcely breathe, struggling in tight maddening circles beneath the smoke hole, unable to escape, unable to alight, flying round and round until the logs themselves began to spin, and Nina, reaching for a pole that wasn't there, saw the dirt floor of the hogan rise up and slap her on the cheek. She pulled her legs up beneath her, arms and legs crouching protectively over the pollen child inside.

Dust crawled like insects through the wetness of her forehead. Far away she heard a little one calling "Mama, mama, come quick, Nina is sick!" Leaves of babble filled the writhing hogan. Coolness licked her thighs as her mother raised her skirt. "Quick, find Johnny," her mother was saying. "Tell him to ride Proud Horse to Uncle Tinker. Tell him we need the pickup right away. We must take Nina to the hospital in Tuba."

Her mother's kneeling face hovered heavy with concern against the blurry backdrop of the logs. Alongside her was Tooter, Naomi's child, frightened and threatening tears as he watched his aunt sprawling in the dirt. Nina raising on an elbow touched the child's forehead, brushing a wisp of hair, and squeezed his small fist in her own; playing a game they often played. The child grinned, and ran, splayfooted, out of the hogan. Nina felt her belly draining into the earth.

Her temple in the dirt knew the tide of evening sheep flowing silently home toward the pens. Footsteps and yelling fainted bleak in the dust. Her mother was saying words. They made no sound.

She closed her eyes against the spinning logs. She did not really believe the eyeless beating wings were the ghost of her father. Still, she trembled. She would not let anyone—any *thing*—steal her baby, and feed it to the dogs.

Not this one.

She squeezed her belly tightly with her elbows. Her mind crossed dried-out fields, to that other hospital, in Santa Fe, a year ago. Her clothes were gone then, and raw as shucked corn she lay inside a nubby gown that reached below her knees beneath a medicine-smelling sheet. The nightgown rested in quiet folds between her legs, the coarse linen touching her warm and sending fine silver wires of smile somewhere deep beneath the pain. Through her belly and breasts and brain the fine wires shivered, handsome boys on spirit ponies bearing gifts. She stretched her ankles and tightened her rear, and the nubby gown all rich with knowhow rubbed its fingers deeper in the warm. Silver tremors ran once more beneath the pain, warriors home from battle with the news, the news she half-knew even while swallowing: that pills in amber bottles were useless remedy against the breaking, muted scream at the fork in the road. She had swallowed near a handful, and seemed still to be alive.

Tentatively, with a gathering of strength, she split her eyelids, not enough to separate the lashes, which clung like brothers and sisters in the dark, but enough to let the bright white light bore in through her eyes, bright white light of day she thought never to see again, and pour through shoulders and thighs into arms and legs, the daylight sailing gently in the vessels of her blood, riding on waves of warmth and fertile tomorrows; restoring her to life. The fork still was there, stretching away like her widespread legs in the bed, it would have to be faced some day, some year, but the great black werewolf of despair, implacable, inescapable, seemed to have vanished, leaving in its place only sleeping yellow dogs, and a careless passing by.

She opened her eyes, slowly, and let them comprehend the morning or afternoon of another chance. The harsh white of first light diffused into a window on the far side of the room, shadowed by the spider branch of an apricot tree. A soft brown bird, she could not see what kind, bobbed easily on a breeze-blown bough, a splintered twig or broken worm in its beak, then startled by some unseen warning leaped away, leaving just the calm recoiling limb, one life where a moment before there had been two.

Eyes glazed, she rolled her head on the pillow, and found the room was larger than she thought. Not far away was another bed, empty, but sitting up

2

as if to eat. She realized she was in a hospital, and with a shudder looked upward at the ceiling, half expecting to see there formless forms of spirits of the dead, drifting and wrestling like guilty gray smoke from cigarettes, wailing snakes of once-was-living, spitting evil juice in shackled rage. But nothing looked down at her but the squash-colored ceiling, peeling in places but still as the desert at noon. They might be invisible, she thought, but felt no evil presence beyond the scorching sage in her throat. Perhaps the spirits of the dead had made their peace at last with the white man's world, which refused to cut holes in hospital walls to let them out. Perhaps the spirits, shriveled souls, had learned to squeeze to their final place through the screens of white men's windows. She would have to ask Grandfather One Blue Eye when she went home.

She had asked him in the summer why her father had died that day. Why her father had died that way, alone, naked, in the sweathouse. He had spoken as always in a frozen poem: "That which we call Life is but a laugh, on the face of a skeleton. One day there is only bones becoming earth, and a useless smile that, screaming, joins the wind, and dwells in the house of others." She had become impatient with the old man, for the only time in her life, insisting: "Yes, but why now, why there?" He had looked with sadness into her eyes, and then into the flames, and said: "He thought the sheep were deer, who could forage for themselves." The riddle had left her more confused than ever. Her mother said One Blue Eye always spoke with the wisdom of the years. Others whispered that it was only peyote talking.

Wearily she closed her lids again, relaxing at the less-pain of the sweatsage cooling off. She drifted in the hammock of wake-or-sleep, drifted for longer than she knew, and thought she heard voices of Anglos somewhere near, the voice of a kitcarson from a deep dark dream of the night before, a kitcarson stuffing a rifle down her throat. The bitter word bubbling up from some festering pool of past dashed her father's sullen image in her face (may his ghost rest easily!) his twisted face spitting kitcarsons like poisoned seeds

3

between his gulps of Coors. She tried once more to forgive him; and again only half succeeded.

Her father's written name was Anderson Yazzie, but it was all but forgotten long ago. He had been known since childhood as Not-So-Fast, because one leg was shorter than the other, and he could not run or climb as well as the other small boys when they were out throwing sticks at rabbits or playing on the mesas. Instead he spent dark brown hours seated like a pet lamb near the legs of his great grandfather, Many Horses, who told in a voice that was dry and rasping the good stories of the time when The People had been more fortunate than now, when they had many sheep and many horses and all the grazing room they would ever need. In those days The People were lords of the earth, feared by all, and Not-So-Fast's eyes grew round as ripe black cherries as he listened to tales of the raids led by Many Horses when he was young, raids on villages of the Pueblo people who lived near the female river. The raids were in late summer, when the fields of the Pueblo people were pregnant with corn and squash and melons, to be carried home along with sheep and horses and young girls to serve for slaves and other uses. After the raids The People would make peace with the Pueblos, and there would be no war through winter and spring, until summer came and the fields were rich again with food, and it was time once more for The People to go and raid, according to their custom. Hearing those stories, Not-So-Fast would see himself on a painted pony as fast as wind, raiding far across the river with a beautiful bow in his hand and a clutch of perfect arrows in a goatskin bag, coming home with fat sheep and sleek horses and baskets filled with fruit, and the whole outfit for miles around holding the Enemy Way for him to cleanse him of the killing and the dirt of foreign people. Excited by his vision, the boy would stand up quickly, and often would fall on his face in the dust of the hogan, tripping over thorns and cactus sleeping in his feet. When that happened the old man Many Horses would heave a croaking laugh.

4

Sometimes the boy would ask why it was that the bellies of The People no longer burst with too much corn and too much mutton. Then all the children would gather round, the brothers and sisters and cousins, and the mothers and fathers, and their brothers and sisters, and even mothers and fathers of the mothers and fathers, and they would sit quietly on the ground near the flickering fire, wrapped in blankets against the evening chill, and listen to the old man Many Horses tell the story they had heard so many times, the story that nested in their muscles and bones, of when the white men rode in from the east and made war against The People, not raids for horses and sheep but bitter endless war without a reason, until The People had nothing to eat but the salt of their tears. The soldier who led the war, Many Horses said, was Ahdilohee—the Rope Thrower—who called himself Kit Carson. Kit Carson said he was a friend of The People, and told them the White Father in Washington wanted them to give up their homes and move to different lands beyond the river. Then when The People would not leave, this Kit Carson came with many soldiers and many guns, and started making war like a witch on horseback. Some of The People left, but most stayed to fight, because this was the land of Changing Woman and Spider Woman and all the Holy People, and they knew that chants and cures would be powerless anywhere else. Not even the pollen from corn would save them; anyplace else they would die. They fought the soldiers bravely, knowing they had never lost a war, but the soldiers kept coming like a river from the east and The People began to fall from their horses, their blood coloring the snow and turning dust into mud. They retreated into the sacred canyons and onto the mesa tops, but Kit Carson's men burned their fields and killed their sheep, and waited through the cold winter nights. Then The People, starving and cold, had nothing left to do but surrender, and march on ragged feet where the white men sent them, three hundred miles away toward the morning sun.

Motionless in the bed, labeled with a plastic hospital tag on her wrist that spelled both her names wrong—Nona Yazz, it said, instead of Nina Yazzie—

traveling the scent of memory tracks to the time of the long dark suffering, to the stories she had heard as a little girl, she felt in her stored-up heart at one again with The People; as she always did in part, as she always would in part no matter how deep she strayed into the strange world of the Anglos, where hurry barked at the sleeping sun and chickens fried in boxes red and white, instead of running scrawny near the hogans for small boys to lasso with their ropes. Bitter and sweet dwelled side by side inside her head, noisy ravens brave and frightened on a burning scarecrow. Like now, when hunger watered her mouth despite the flames that burned her throat; and instead of wishing for death she found herself wanting Kentucky Fried; or even "candy-for-Nina," her war cry as a child.

She opened her eyes, wondering what food she would get in this medi-cine place. And closed them against the bright. And thought again of the Long Walk, the story they all knew, the story her father had learned too well at the feet of the old man. With few horses and few wagons The People had had to march. Many were killed by hunger or thirst along the way. Those who didn't die were kept in a small place, and their bodies used to roaming far among the painted canyons and rugged mesas withered and became ill, sickened by strange food and new water and loneliness that sat inside them like wounded birds. The passing time was like pinon logs piling on their backs until they would break. They did not understand why the White Father Lincoln wanted it so. For four timeless years they lived as low as snakes, in holes in the ground covered with branches and leaves, far from Dinetlah. Some of the woman gave themselves to the soldiers, to get more food to eat. Then word came that they could return, and those who had not died set off on the long walk home. Many Horses himself had made the first Long Walk, his name become a mockery like a stone around his neck, after watching from high on a cliff in Canyon de Chelly as Kit Carson's men chopped down all the peach trees in the canyon, and burned all the hogans, and slaughtered the horses and sheep and left them out to rot. His wife Smiling Woman tried to make soup from bones they found on the cliff, but watching the killing below they couldn't eat a bowl, and three days later they climbed through the snow and surrendered. Many Horses lost his brothers and sisters and two of his children to the hunger and disease, and on the march back with his bones peeking out through once-smooth skin he had only Smiling Woman and his daughter Yellow Peach and his youngest son Far-From-Home, who was an infant sucking at Smiling Woman's breast. For many days they walked, looking toward the sacred place far across the desert. One day a band of Mexicans came galloping on horseback, and attacked the weary marchers. The soldiers there to protect them were few and scattered far. The bandits took those they wanted, and galloped away like ghosts. One of those they took was Smiling Woman. They pulled her baby from her breast, and threw him off a cliff. Many Horses reached home with only the one daughter by his side. He never heard news of Smiling Woman after that.

The Long Walk. A way of the earth by now, as much as the sheep in the pens and the water in the springs and the four places deep below the crust. As well to claw at it now as bite a bear in the dark. But not so with her father Not-So-Fast. When the old man Many Horses finished his tale the eyes of all who heard would be heavy once again with bitter water, but the little boy was scalded by his tears. He stumbled wildly outside the hogan, crying through the darkness that he would get his bow and arrows and shoot dead this kitcarson through the heart. Once his brother Eddie shouted after him, "You better make yourself some long arrows, my little brother, to kill someone what's dead a hunnerd years." The joke and laughter bounced away in the dark, but this word this one word kitcarson was branded in his brain as with an iron. Years later when his leg hurt bad and he could not do his share at the sheep dipping and turned instead to the whiskey and the Coors, his anger flew like arrows at the eyes of kitcarsons. All the Anglos he had never met in worlds he had never seen at the ends of roads he had never traveled that led off the reservation, all these were hated kitcarsons who bowed his neck with

7

troubles. Anglos who crossed the reservation in shiny cars, buying beads for spoiled children left at home, they too were kitcarsons, to be spit at behind their backs. When her mother's brother Tinker Begay first took his jeep to Kayenta, to be a guide to Anglos visiting the valley, Not-So-Fast sneered at him, though not to his face, that he was licking the shoes of the kitcarsons. Eating a red licorice stick she asked her Uncle Tinker about that, and he said there was good and bad in all people, and that while some of the Anglos might be mostly bad others were not. The suffering of the timeless time must never happen again, he said, but the people today could not be blamed for it, even if the government still was deaf and dumb. This was the same thing her teacher had said in school, and coming from Uncle Tinker it made good sense. So in the summer and on weekends when she was not in school or busy with the sheep, she loved to ride in the jeep with him as he took a group of Anglos through the valley for fifteen dollars each. She would take the bag of candy and apples the Anglos gave her (she knew her Uncle Tinker made them buy it), and when they reached the hogan she would share it with her brothers and sister who came running out to see. As the jeep rolled up her mother Alice Yazzie would stop whatever she was doing and quickly crouch beside her loom, so the Anglos could see what they wanted to see, a Navajo woman weaving. They had to get their moneysworth, so they would tell their friends to come. Afterward the Anglos would take pictures of her and her mother and her little brothers and sister standing barefoot outside the hogan. When they asked Uncle Tinker if they had to pay to take the pictures, he would say no, but it would be nice if they bought some beads from the little girl. She would show them the beads she had made, and they each would buy a strand or two and put them around their necks. The Anglos would be happy because they didn't have to pay to take the pictures, and she and her mother would be happy because picture-taking in the valley cost fifty cents, and for the beads which were worth a dime they had got two dollars apiece. The Anglos would admire the hogan, and the rug her mother was weaving, and

8

the children, and the sheep, and the dogs, and anything else that was lying around, as if all of these were strange and wonderful things, and then everybody would say goodbye to everybody, and Uncle Tinker would take the Anglos away in his jeep to show them the rest of the valley. Only then would her father Not-So-Fast come out of the storage hogan, where he had been hiding for half an hour, too proud to be seen by the Anglos. "Kitcarsons," he would mutter below his breath, as if it was a curse, and then if her mother was feeling happy she would give him a dollar from the bead money to go off and buy some Coors. Selling liquor on the reservation was against the white man's law, but her father could always get it in Kayenta. She never knew where till after the day he died.

Like a breeze slipping under a door the air in the room was stirring near her face. Thirsty, divining a hovering, wishing water, she opened her eyes. An unknown man was standing near the bed. "Good morning," he said. "Or I should say, good afternoon. How're you feeling today?" The voice of midnight's kitcarson, who unlocked with pain her father's terrible word. She didn't speak, but stared at him, her eyes dull caves of anger and of fear. The man spoke again, as if she had replied. "You must have one sore throat. Would you like some water?"

He was wearing brown Levis, and a plaid shirt open at the neck, a T-shirt peeping out. He had a pen in his breast pocket, and a sandcast Navajo buckle on his belt. His face was handsome with deep dark eyes, a solid chin, and rumpled brown hair that curled at the ends. Without waiting for an answer he moved to a table near the bed, and poured water into a glass from a cracked yellow pitcher. He did not look at all like her mother's brother Tinker, but something in his manner reminded her. She took the glass he was offering, lifted her head and propping on an elbow sipped slowly. The water trickled the sandy sage like melting snow in spring. She sipped again, then gave him the glass and let her head fall back to the sighing safety of the pillow.

9

"I'm Dr. Kirschbaum," the man said. "I'm afraid it was me who pumped your stomach last night. We had to put a tube in your throat. That's what hurt it so. It should be okay in another day or two."

Flushes of shame dipped her body in a sweathouse. Her eyes found the blank white of the sheet. She spoke into her chest softly. "Was I going to die?"

"That's hard to say, Nina."

The sound of her name pecked at her breast like a crow. Her dark eyes darted up.

"We couldn't take the chance. We didn't know how much you had taken. It's possible you would have recovered. There was no way to tell."

Her eyes returned to the sheet. Her father and the other dead were leading her down the steep dry sandy path, to the underground of nothing. A chill motionless wind replaced the sweathouse.

"Let's have a look at you," the doctor said.

He pulled a screeching curtain around the bed, though there was no one else in the room, and raising the sheet at the bottom pressed with firm but gentle fingertips her ankles and her legs. He dropped the sheet and took from his black bag drooping on a wooden chair a silver pen with a light on the end, and looked with the light deep into her eyes, pulling back the lids with practiced fingers, and down into her throat. With doctor's rubber wires in his ears he listened to her heartbeat and her back. Her heart always nervous with doctors was beating the banging of drums at the Enemy Way. She thought she ought to explain, but there wasn't a need.

"You're fine," the doctor said, straightening up. "Your throat is red, but that should take care of itself. I'd like you to rest here for another day. Tomorrow we'll probably check you out."

His words hesitated, a hummingbird at a flower; then continued, less certainly. "Do you plan to go back to school?"

Her mind still was wandering at her ankles. She nodded.

10

"I'd like to talk to you," the doctor said.

He put his black bag on the floor and turned the wooden chair, and strad-dled it, the back of the chair between his legs, an Anglo riding a mule. Before he could speak, she did.

"Why did you look at my feet?"

Her eyes were on his face, and he returned the gaze. For a hanging in-stant like a drawn-out blink they weren't doctor and patient, but equals, facing each other across the broad dry wash of ancient challenge. His eyes not wavering, the doctor said: "Shouldn't I have?"

The moment hung two heartbeats longer before she quietly said yes, and conceded her eyes to the sheet. He was the doctor again, she was again the girl of seventeen. But somewhere inside her, apathy started to melt, and water the roots of respect. He was young, this doctor, but he seemed to know some things. He knew that to examine the head first, the way most doctors did, was to reverse the natural order, and bring evil spirits down upon the patient. The proper way was always to start with the feet.

"Nina" —some slight pain in his voice compelled her attention— "they want to expel you from school."

A moment before she might have put on the mask of not caring she wore so well at school. But now, because of the feet, because of his easy manner, the empty, hazy gulf that often spread between herself and her life wasn't there.

"Because I took the pills?"

"Because of the pills, the cutting of classes, the not finishing your as-signments. . ."

She lowered her eyes again. Maybe he knew too much, this medicine man.

"You don't have to worry," he said. "I won't let them expel you. I told them that if they did, you would probably go back to the reservation and kill

11

yourself. And that it would be their fault. I told them I was going to write that in my report. They get frightened about things like that."

She kept her eyes on her knees below the sheet. She wished she was back on the reservation, alone out in the valley, sitting in a hollow of rock where the sun never reached and the lonely coolness kissed her face when she came to draw and keep it company, and eagles rode the brightness atop the cliff, far above the caring.

"Why did you do that?"

The doctor rested his chin on his hands on the back of the chair, a brooding student grown older. "I'm not sure. Maybe it's because I don't like to see talent go to waste. I went over to the school this morning, and looked at some of your paintings. They're very good."

Through the window beyond the bed another bird was clutching the spider tree. It rode the windy bough hearing nothing; like the children on the seesaws up the road, at the school for the deaf. Staring she saw the branches of the tree become dark, treacherous forks, a fork in every twig, beckoning.

"I'm sorry," she said. "What did you say?"

"I said I want to make a deal with you. I stuck my neck out for you today. I'm willing to keep doing that. But only if you want me to. Only if you want to go to classes, and work at your painting, and stop messing around. There are problems, I know. Otherwise you wouldn't be here. Some of them maybe I can guess at. Others, nobody knows but you."

He ran his hand through his rumpled hair, trying to press it smooth; a gesture he must have had since he was a boy.

"My office is right down the hall. When you go back to school, whenever you have a problem, whenever you need to talk about something, even if you're just feeling lonely, why don't you come by the office, and we'll talk. I'm not a head doctor. We'll just talk, like friends. A lot of times that helps. More than you might think."

She listened, and said nothing. The doctor uncurled from the chair and stood, placing the chair where it had been against the wall. "You don't have to decide now," he said. "Just rest today and think about what I said. I'll be back in the morning."

When he was gone she lay again with her eyes closed. She was worn smooth, as if she had been in the sun too long with the sheep, and had wandered too far to get back before noon to the pens and the flowing shade. Like a dog gnawing at a stick she wondered about this doctor what's-his-name (she would have to ask the nurse.) There were things inside her she had never told to anyone; certainly not to the teachers and counselors at the school, whose phrases came out of books, who talked of "adjusting to the white world" as if it meant putting milk in your morning coffee. She had adjusted, all right. By hiding her feelings with masks; by turning stubbornness into withdrawal. Rebellion had become a passive art; cutting classes, skipping assignments, not painting; academic suicide. Of all the students at the school, only with Robert had she felt free and natural. Only Robert seemed to understand. But he was gone like yesterday, back home in South Dakota, or at college in the East, she did not even know. She was glad she had not told him about the baby. . . the not baby. . . Still, a letter would have been nice. Smooth hands of Robert.

Her muscles spoke from laying in the bed. She turned the sheet, swung her legs, wriggled feet into slippers that someone had left on the floor, padded shakily to the bathroom beyond a door in the corner of the room. When she had finished and washed her hands she peered into a mirror on the medicine chest. Her shiny black hair, hanging to her waist, felt knotted, but she couldn't find a comb. She rubbed her face, her high cheekbones, her Chinese eyes. Grandfather One Blue Eye believed The People had come up to the surface of the earth long ago through a hole in the sky below. The schoolbooks said they had journeyed over the top of the world from China. Perhaps there wasn't a conflict, perhaps they both were right; but her almond-

13

shaped eyes sided with the schoolbooks. She smoothed her hair with her hands, midnight sky of hair from which her face peered not red, as the white men used to say, not leather or copper dusk, as Tinker's or her father's; more a tawny, burnished mooncolor, scrubbed aglow amid the midnight sky. She let it fall and pulled the gray hospital gown tight over her breasts, and in at her narrow waist, eyes still in the mirror. She did not think of herself as pretty. Her hair was too black, too thick, too straight, the structure of her face too visible, her skin neither golden brown like that of some Indian girls, nor the pale pink-white of models in magazines. But she knew that others, looking at her, saw beauty. She could see from the corners of her eyes heads turning and eyes following her when she walked through the downtown Plaza, even if she was wearing only her usual jeans and a sweater or a blouse. When she sat in the school gallery practicing drawing by copying photographs she could sense the tourists nudging one another with their elbows; pointing her out, not because she was Indian—the campus was criss-crossed with Indian boys and girls—but because of some vision of beauty of theirs into which she seemed to fit. Once, a wrinkled, gray-haired lady who was a well-known photographer had come up to her and told her how beautiful she was; had said it not as flattery or condescension, but with a certain purity; the way one might speak to a flower in the desert. The boys at school liked to look at her, of course, and she was glad of that, but some of them would have liked to look at a she-goat. It was a bother, sometimes, when she wanted to be alone. More and more these past two months, since returning to school from the reservation, she had wanted to be alone.

She padded back and sat on the bed, thinking again of the doctor. Absently, she removed the slippers; and then, with a clutch of horror, stared at them. The left one had been on her right foot, the right one had been on her left foot: an omen of death.

She dropped the slippers as if they were rattlesnakes, and curled up on the bed, bent, tight, fetal, a knot in her stomach. Voices in the hall outside

14

frightened her; then, as they continued, soothed her. Superstition, they would call it here; she had to adjust.

Perhaps, if cures and chants were powerless beyond the four sacred mountains, then omens might be, too. The thought was calming. Her muscles loosened; she stretched her legs in the bed; and after a time fell into a sleep whose dreams she wouldn't remember. But first she reached to the floor, and placed the slippers right side up alongside each other, the right on the right side, the left on the left; as is the natural order.

*****

Strong hands were lifting her out of the dust, wrapping her in a blanket. "Get her shoes," her mother's voice was saying. Out of the darkness and into the light she floated on muscles and chest, and was lowered onto something hard, something shaking, like the rattle of an engine.

"Seven months?" a voice was saying—it was her mother's brother Tinker's— "Maybe she'll just have her baby, and it will come out fine."

Metal doors clanged shut and engine noises changed, and with her mother crouched nearby the hard bottom bucked through the sand like a bronc, the jumping breeze bracing her sweaty brow. Sprays of sand scratched at the bottom as the tires jounced in the furrows that passed in the valley for a road. A sprig of sunlight warmed her face, then disappeared below the side of the truck. It was late afternoon, she remembered. She had been cooking stew for dinner when the eagle broke her sac.

"Ride to Kayenta, to Holiday Inn," her mother was saying over the side. "Have Mr. Watkins call the hospital at Tuba, Tell them we're bringing Nina to have her baby. Tell them we'll be there in an hour."

She heard Johnny urge the pony, but the sound of the trot was smothered by the suffering of the engine. She squeezed her belly tight beneath the blanket as the pickup bounced and bumped along the dirt.

15

Her baby. Robert's baby. Not Robert's, that was last year, when the blood came, and the dog. She wrenched her head to the side, so she wouldn't vomit on herself; but nothing came; just a dry hurting heave.

"Are you all right?" her mother said.

Not Robert's but that other, the child of swimming fish. No matter. She would make it Michael's, if she wanted. A girl was allowed to pretend. That's what babies were for.

She wondered what her father had pretended. Which was the trembling real, and which the sickly pretend. She knew so well the story of her birth. Knew it much too well, for all those years. So well the images burned in her mind's eye, images she had heard but never seen. Her mother in the hogan, deep in labor, wrinkled Good With Children at her side. Her proud father mounting his horse, trotting off in the purple of waning day, going hunting, to bring back meat to celebrate his son. For miles he hunted amid the sagebrush and the pinons along the slopes of the mesas in the sinking twilight, without any luck. Then, as darkness gathered and he turned toward home, he saw a wolf in bushes to the left. He raised his rifle and fired, and heard a howl, and knew he had hit. He rode to the bush to get the wolf—but couldn't see it. He peered under blankets of dark, pushing back branches that clung and grabbed at his shirt. Still, he couldn't find the wolf. Slowly, then faster, terror began to rise inside his heart. He kicked the horse with his good leg and galloped, frantic, through the darkness, back to the hogan. The horse's mouth was white with foam, and Not-So-Fast's eyes were wild and wide with fear. Trembling, he limped inside, and fell to the ground beside the pale green fire.

"Look, my husband," his wife Alice said. She was lying on a sheepskin, wrapped in a blanket, a swaddled baby cradled in her arm. "Come look at your first-born daughter, Nina Yazzie."

16

Not-So-Fast looked toward the voice, but his eyes blinded by the fire saw nothing. His voice was dead as he spoke. "I think I killed a wolf man," he said.

The hogan was quiet, except for the popping of the logs. He told her what had happened. "Maybe you missed the wolf," Alice said. "Maybe you wounded it, and it ran away in the dark."

"Maybe," Not-So-Fast said. But when she offered him his newborn girl to hold, he refused. He was too nervous, he said. He was afraid he might drop the child.

Soon after the relatives came, to celebrate the birth. There was much joking and drinking, and happy nods at the beauty of the child. "Brother-in-law," Alice's brother Joseph said," a goat has conceived a lilac. Are you sure the baby is yours?" Not-So-Fast joined the laughter, drinking from a bottle. He rarely drank, but on this night led the others. What better night for a man to get drunk than the birth of a healthy first-born?

As lateness came the party moved to the hogan of Tinker Begay, while Alice and the baby slept. Not-So-Fast drank till the last of them left, then limped home, fearful beneath the liquor and the stars, and lay near the dying fire. Alice, waking when he entered, watched with troubled eyes her husband's arms and legs twitch and jerk in his sleep, as if pawed by a bear.

The strong voice of Tinker, singing the morning chant as he let the sheep from the pens, wakened Not-So-Fast at dawn. The chirping of birds in the cottonwoods tolled in his head like the bells of missionaries. Light cleaved his brain, a streak of wild dogs attacking sheep. Ignoring the pain, he stumbled outside, found his horse tied to a bush, mounted, and started toward the slopes, saying nothing; forgetting even his coffee. When he reached the region of the wolf he found the bush he thought was the one, and dropped to the ground. There was blood on the lower branches, and blood on the earth. He followed the dry brown drops in among other bushes, then across an open space to a juniper that stood alone in a clearing. At the base of the juniper, the trail of blood disappeared.

Not-So-Fast circled the tree. The tracks of the injured wolf went no further. Frantically he looked about. Then he saw the tracks of a barefoot girl, faint in the hard earth under the tree, unmistakable further out in the sand. The tracks led toward a ridge a hundred yards away. The sun was barely up, but Not-So-Fast's sweaty clothes clung to him like disease. He felt dizzy with fear and afterdrink. He wanted to sit in the shade of the tree and sleep, but dared not go near the laughing juniper. He wanted to get on his horse and ride till there was a hundred years between him and the sacred mountains. He wanted to visit Changing Woman in her guest house by the sea, to rest in her arms and be caressed and never have to care. Like her sons, he would vanquish monsters ... if only he wasn't afraid.

For a time he couldn't move. Then, slowly, his rifle poised in both hands, he began to follow the tracks. He followed till he was ten feet short of the ridge, then lay on his belly and crawled the rest of the way. Only his eyes and forehead peered above the top.

The far side of the ridge sloped away to a sandy wash. At the edge of the wash stood one lonely hogan, with smoke ascending. Not-So-Fast knew of the place. An old couple lived there, alone with their granddaughter. There were no relatives, no family, no outfit. Just the three of them. They were friendly with no one in the valley.

Not- So-Fast wanted to run the other way. But he needed like poisoned hunger to find the truth. Slowly he stood, rifle ready, and followed the tracks down toward the hogan. He expected dogs to bark at his approach. But there seemed to be none. Nothing barked but the silence.

Unhindered, he entered the hogan. An old man and an old woman were squatting on the dirt. Between them, on a sheepskin, lay a dark-haired girl, about fourteen years old. Her eyes were closed.

18

The old people took no notice of Not-So-Fast, until he spoke. "I'm looking for my dog, Old Yellow," he said. "He's been gone three days."

Lined as winter wood, the old man raised his eyes, vacant in a used-up stare. Vaguely he shook his head. Then he looked down again.

"The girl," Not-So-Fast said, nodding toward the sick child. "What's the matter?"

The woman spoke without seeing. Once, long ago, she could have been the old man's twin. "Someone shot her."

Not-So-Fast's knees turned to river, his rifle to rope, coiling, hissing, spitting. The woman, hearing or not hearing, spoke in cracked leather. "You hunted last night?"

A head shook no on the neck of Not- So-Fast. "My daughter was born last night. Big party. No one left the hogan."

The woman nodded, and looked again at the girl.

"How is she?" Not-So-Fast said. Then, with confidence: "She'll get well."

"Our granddaughter is dead," the old man said.

"Now you have a daughter, and we do not," the woman said. Her voice was gray as sage.

Not-So-Fast stood rooted, struck by black lightning, clouds of terror rolling in over a copper monument. *Chindi!* The hogan was *Chindi!* He turned and ran, screaming, out of the hogan and up toward the ridge, swinging his leg, choking on his yells, chasing his own ghost. His bad leg caught in a hole, his ankle twisted, he fell to the ground. He scrambled up and kept running, sand in his rifle, sharp cutting pains in his leg. Over the ridge he ran, rocking, past whispering bushes, to where his horse was waiting. With both hands he threw his rifle as far as he could into the bushes up the slope of the mesa. Then he mounted and kicked the horse and galloped like the night before, as fast as he could, back through the valley.

19

Breathless and shaking, he summoned Alice and her brothers, Joseph and Tinker, and One Blue Eye, and told them what had happened. He had killed a werewolf, he said. The two old people, they must be witches, he said, to be sitting in the hogan with the dead. There was bad pain in his leg. The witches, or the ghost of the wolf girl, had put a curse on his leg.

He found a bottle from the night before, and swallowed to still the pain. The others were frightened, and full of sympathy. The men led Not-So-Fast to the sweathouse, and they all took sweat baths, chanting chants, inviting the Holy People to join them, to wash away the evil, to purify the life. When they emerged they rolled in the sand, and doused one another with water. Afterward Alice brought the new baby to Not-So-Fast, to cheer him; to lift his thoughts from what had happened. He refused to touch the infant. "The ghost is in me," he said. "It is not for me to touch her."

His leg continued to hurt. More and more he took drinks to quiet the pain. After a month a Singer was sent for, Hosteen Navajo, the most famous Singer in the region, 85 years old then, in his last years. Hosteen Navajo arrived on a rickety wagon drawn by a sagging white horse. (He was rich enough to have young horses, someone said, but this old white mare was his favorite; besides, he did not want to show off his wealth.) He brought with him only his buckskin medicine bag filled with feathers, herbs, sacred stones and sticks. For four days and four nights Hosteen Navajo sang the Moving Up Way for Not-So-Fast, to rid him of the ghost. When the four days ended, Not-So-Fast's leg felt better, and the outfit exulted like spring. They waved a grateful goodbye as the white-haired old Singer rode his wagon out of the valley, the rear of the wagon crowded now with the four full-grown sheep that were his fee.

Two weeks later, the pain came again. Not-So-Fast said the ghost of the wolf girl still twisted claws in his leg. The people in the outfit began to look at him, wondering. If Hosteen Navajo could not rid him of the ghost, some of them thought, then something was wrong inside.

He began drinking all the time. The drinking and the pain slackened his herding of the cattle. Never would he touch his baby girl.

Her father. Whose eyes were black as burned wood. With a red handkerchief tied around his forehead, the headband always looking too tight, as if it would cut the flow of blood to his brain; as if it had stopped his scalp from falling off in some long-dead massacre by the whites. Turquoise eardrops (when they were not in the safe at the trading post, pawned for whiskey money); his coal-black hair tied neatly in a chongo by her mother, till the later years, when she wouldn't bother, and his hair hung loose. Her father, who was there and wasn't, who slept in the furthest corner of the hogan, who herded the cattle on horseback, except when he was bored and left them to Tinker and got odd jobs in Kayenta, cutting logs or stacking cinder blocks for a new store or a new house; weaving up the road in the pickup hours after work, with the drink in him, careening the pickup in the rut tracks too fast to stop for any stray sheep or child (though he never hit any), hurtling the truck to make up for the lameness in his leg; swerving into soft pockets of sand at the side of the road, the pickup caught like a rabbit in a trap, wheels spinning sand in hysterical boredom, then without warning lurching forward, a foul meat upchucked; dogs and scrawny chickens scattering as the pickup hit the hard rock-strewn dirt around the hogan, and slammed to a stop; her father climbing down, a crippled bird walking. Or going off to Window Rock for weeks at a time, to visit his family, whom he didn't like, for the sake of what people would say. Her father, whose life revolved in tight uneven circles around the leg that made him limp; his right leg, shorter, thinner, paler than the other, causing his shoulder to dip with every step he took, his right shoulder, bobbing like a duck. Never in his life had he walked on level ground, nor ever would. He did not drag the leg, but swung it forward in a broken arc, forever stepping in holes that weren't there; doomed like a horse with a splintered foreleg to wince till death on the weight of it; in good times thrusting his head high in defiant affirmation; in bad times bemoaning in

21

drink and anger the misfortune he had carried from the womb. Her father. Who never once hugged her close with love; who never sat her on his knee and played with her; who turned his eyes away, as if she were a mother-in-law, instead of his first-born daughter; whose secret torment she could not understand until she herself was a woman; until he was dead. Her father; whom she wished had been a father.

*****

Tears were playing leapfrog on Nina's cheeks. The pickup, grinding up a short, sandy hill, bucked over the top, onto a level. Her mother, seeing the tears, stroked Nina's hair. "We're on the highway now," she said. "There will be less bumps, less pain." Nina felt for her mother's legs, and snuggled her head into her lap. The tears ran quicker still.

"It's a good hospital at Tuba," her mother said, squeezing her shoulder. "They'll take good care of you, and the baby."

Nina nuzzled her head, wiping tears in the folds of blanket, thinking: It is a good hospital at Tuba. Michael said so. Michael worked there two years, before moving to Santa Fe. Sweet, wise, frightened Michael.

She could hardly remember why she had gone to him. She who had learned in her father's house to trust no stranger, least of all an Anglo. It had been something about his eyes, set deep amid his strong features, a sadness in his eyes, even when he smiled, that seemed to reflect her own. Impulse had led her the first time. Pausing at the steps of the dorm, a fork, a tiny fork, she envisioned her roommate loneliness waiting upstairs, and turned for once the other way, art books still in hand, and crossed the asphalt parking lot that separated the Indian school from the Indian hospital. A Cochiti family sat on the steps, waiting anxiously. She nodded and passed inside, down a color-drained corridor, and found his office. He wasn't there, but a hurrying nurse said he would soon be back, that she could wait. She set her books on the edge of a desk covered with white papers and folders the color of straw, and looked about. A steel cabinet with a glass door was crammed with ominous medical books. On top was a gold statue of a jumping man, a basketball in his hands. A window on the far side slatted with Venetian blinds looked across a sparse lawn to a wire fence, and beyond it to traffic passing. Along-side the desk she saw her face in the glass of black-framed papers on the wall. Papers with curly black writing, words she didn't understand, another language. The words made her nervous. She was sorry she had come. There was nothing she could talk about here.

She thought of leaving but the doctor came brushing through the door, and tossed a clip-board on the desk. "I'm glad you came, I was starting to give up hope," he said, and motioned to a chair beside the desk; but she did not want to sit. Answering her glance he explained the papers on the wall. They were from the schools he went to, Arizona State, and the University of New York, and a hospital with a pretty name, View of Bells, where he treated not Navajos but poor whites, and poor blacks, and Spanish from an island in the sea, that were known as Chicano Ricans. He himself was Navajo, he said. "Kirsch means cherry. Baum means tree. Michael Cherry Tree." She grinned.

When he motioned to the seat again, she sat. He sat too, in a swivel chair behind the desk, and lit a cigarette from a crumpled pack on the desk, and offered her one, which she didn't take. He asked how she was doing since she went back to school after the pills, and she said a lot better, she was painting again and going to all her classes. But you're still lonely he asked, reading her face, and she admitted "a little," that her best friend from last year was gone and she had no one to talk to, she didn't like the counselors and she felt they didn't like her. Will you talk to me he said, but she wasn't ready yet. Instead she asked him what his name was when it wasn't Navajo. It's Jewish he said. There must have been a funny look on her face because she had never seen one before.

23

He lowered his head like a bull about to charge and rumpled his rumpled hair and said, "See, no horns." She was puzzled, and flipped the pages of an art book from the pile till she came to the picture she wanted, and showed it to him. Moses with horns on his head. The doctor nodded—don't call me doctor call me Mike, you're Nina I'm Mike he said—and explained about the horns, Moses came down from the mountain with the rays of God coming out of his head, but the Hebrew word for rays is a lot like the word for horns. Michaelangelo had made a mistake.

He gave her back the book and put his feet up on the desk like no doctor she had ever seen, and instead of pressing her to talk the way the counselors did he said he had a theory: that even if she never met one before there was a lot in common between Navajos and Jews. He told her his theory, how the Navajos call themselves The People and the Jews call themselves The Chosen People, which is the same thing, how they both have sacred lands, Dinetlah and Palestine, even the same kind of land, a desert. When they make movies about Palestine he said they often film them on the Navajo reservation. She didn't know that but told him the movie *Stagecoach* was made right near her house, before she was born. His head nearly flew to the ceiling when she said that. "You live in Monument Valley?" he said, as if it was a part of the sky and the mesas were made of candy or chocolate cake. "That's my favorite place in the whole world." Her grandfather One Blue Eye had been in the movie, she told him, or said he had been in the movie, but when she saw it on TV once at her friend Annie's house in Kayenta she couldn't find him. She asked her mother if Grandfather One Blue Eye would tell a lie, and her mother said never, but that his face was so ugly it broke the camera, and they left him out. Her mother would say this only when Grandfather One Blue Eye could hear, and he would stalk out of the hogan, making believe he was mad, and someone would have to go out and coax him back.

The doctor laughed. His face was softer, even more handsome, when he laughed. The old people are strong he said. Tradition, maybe that's what we

24

both have. Maybe that's what helps us survive. They tried to wipe out the Navajos—Kit Carson's men—and they tried the same with the Jews. "He Who Smells His Own Moustache," she said, remembering from school. But we both survived, he said. The Mormons in Utah believe the Navajos are actually descended from the Lost Tribe of Israel. "How did they get lost?" she asked. He grinned and said, "Probably looking for their sheep." She grinned, too.

He had a way of making a joke, of making her smile, in the midst of a serious talk, and it made her feel relaxed. The tenseness she had felt when she walked into the office had flown out the window into the air. She felt safe being there. She liked the way he talked, as if he cared about what he was saying, and wanted her to care. As if she were adult, the same as him, not like the teachers at school. As if he were her friend. His look warmed her body. Not like the he-goat look of the boys at school, which turned her to stone.

"How come you know so much about the Navajos?" she said, and he told her he had worked at the hospital in Tuba for two years. He loved it there he said, it was so different from New York City where the dirt grew high in the air. After work he would go walking in the desert, watching the moon change the shape of the rocks, and maybe seeing an eagle overhead. That's what life should be all about, he said. Watching nature at work. She asked why he had left, and he said because of his wife. That she was bored, and wanted to go back to New York, where there was more busy things to do. So they both gave in a little, and moved to Santa Fe. She asked if his wife liked Santa Fe better. She liked it for a year, he said, then she got bored again.

"She went back to New York two months ago," he said. "We're separated now."

She was sorry she had asked, she told him she was sorry for being rude. He shrugged his shoulders, which looked solid over his lean chest, lean she guessed from playing basketball like the golden statue jumping. The telephone on the desk buzzed, and he answered it and then looked at his watch and said dammit he was late he had to check his patients, but he made her promise now that he was finished babbling to come back tomorrow and talk about herself. She liked talking with him, it made her feel good inside. She said she would.

He walked with her to the doorway and then she walked alone down the corridor, her books against her breast. A nurse in white was pushing a man in a wheelchair whose face was covered with bandages. She smiled without thinking into the faceless head; smiling at the doctor's full name. At Michael's full name. Doctor Michael Cherry Tree Without No Horns

*****

Like angry geese the horns of cars were honking. Nina's bones vibrated at a loud answering blast. "What's wrong, mama?" she said. Uncle Tinker rarely was impatient.

Her mother, still seated, was peering over the side of the truck. Her blanket had fallen from her shoulders, from her red velvet blouse. The skin of her neck was taut. The sun had newly set, and the rose-colored sky gave her face a softer hue. So pretty, after five children! A squash-blossom hung around her neck, her favorite, with the large male turquoise. Over it hung two strands of turquoise beads, with joclas. Bracelets hid her wrists. Her finest conchas circled her velvet waist. To impress them at Tuba, Nina knew. So they would be treated well.

"There's sheep on the road," her mother said. "They don't want to move."

The truck was idling. Nina raised her head, and pulled herself carefully onto her knees, holding the side of the truck, her belly in delicate balance. Evening gray was settling over the desert. Fifty yards down the highway glared the bright beams of a car, and behind it another, waiting, honking. Between the cars and the pickup were perhaps a hundred sheep, frozen,

26

carved of stone. A teenaged boy was running about, yelling at the sheep. They wouldn't budge.

No light was coming from the truck. Tinker had cut the beams, in case it was the headlights that had mesmerized the herd. But the sheep still weren't moving. The dumb beasts had claimed the useless asphalt.

Tinker switched on the lights, and the sheep flared yellow. He leaned out the window of the cab, and twisted over his shoulder. "Hold tight, daughter," he said. "We're goin' off the road."

Nina gripped the side of the truck with her hands and forearms and elbows. The pickup plunged and jounced into a broad soft ditch that sided the road, and hurtled through it, a bucking horse, fearful of getting trapped. The truck passed below and around the stonefaced sheep, Tinker shouting curses, then chugged back onto the highway. The truck slowed, and Tinker leaned out the window.

"Everything okay?"

Nina, one hand clutching her belly, waved to him. The wind cooled her wet face in the gathering speed. As she lowered herself beside her mother they could still hear Tinker, calling the sheep coyotes.

"With our sheep we were created," her mother intoned softly.

A hint of smile was playing near her lips. Nina hugged her shoulders, and kissed her cheek. It was fourteen years since her mother first told her that.

*****

Her earliest memory. Chasing chickens through the dirt, running into the corral, waving and shouting at the sheep, helping as they were brought into the pens, then her cousin Naomi Begay saying, "We're having mutton tonight, let's go watch," and taking her by the hand and leading her to the shade, where her mother and Naomi's mother Maria were kneeling under the

27

branches of juniper, and a lone sheep was eating a clump of sage. As she and Naomi watched, holding hands, her small fist clutching a chocolate bar, their mothers grabbed the feet of the sheep, and pushed in onto its side, and tied its ankles with rope. Maria Begay took a blackened frying pan and pushed it under the head and neck of the sheep. "Why did you tie the sheep?" she asked. Her mother didn't answer, but took a short curved knife from the folds of her wide purple skirt. With one hand she held the head of the bleating sheep. With the other, with a quick, sharp pull, she cut its throat. "Mama!" she shrieked, as blood spurted and streamed in a torrent into the frying pan. The twisting sheep shuddered, and fell still. She was crying, and wanted to run away, but Naomi held tight to her hand, and started mocking her. Sniffling in her sobs she watched as the two mothers hung the sheep on the limb of a tree, and cut off all its skin. When that was done Maria took the bloody sheep away. Her mother took the skin and stretched it, driving pegs into the ground to hold it tight. She scraped the fat off the inside, and rubbed dirt into it, to dry the leftover fat and blood.

Smearfaced from chocolate and tears she watched for a time, then wandered off, and sat behind the hogan, trembling. The world had turned to winter; had gone from sun to daddy's kitcarson. She sulked alone, refusing to join in the children's games; punching a dog that playfully licked her face. She would not eat lunch. Only the crackly smell of mutton roasting on the fire induced her to eat her dinner. Roast mutton was a special treat. It tasted good.

After dinner she sat on the ground, watching her mother weave. Her mother was the best weaver in the valley. Sometimes the man at the trading post gave them forty dollars for a single rug. She was still sulking, saddened that hands that could weave so pretty could kill a sheep, when finishing a line her mother put aside the yarn, and sat her on her lap, to make her understand.

"With our sheep we were created," her mother said. "Without The People, all the sheep would die. They would be killed by bears, and coyotes, and

28

packs of wild dogs. In the winter, when snow covers the grass, they would have nothing to eat. The People take care of the sheep, protecting them from their enemies, making sure they have enough to eat. In return, the sheep give The People wool to weave rugs from, and soft furry skins to sleep on; and sometimes food to eat."

"Why can't we just eat mutton?" she said.

Her mother ignored the question. "If we did not kill some of the sheep, there would not be enough grass for the others to eat. We don't kill them for harm, only because we love them. Always remember, little daughter. With our sheep we were created."

She had fallen asleep soon after, safe again in her mother's arms. It was months later before she realized that mutton didn't come from the trading post. By then she didn't care.

*****

The truck was speeding smooth in a rhythmic hum. The sky was dark gray, except for a thin ribbon of yellow white that lined the low horizon to the west. Not a light or a hogan was visible on either side of the road. Early stars were up, those that couldn't sleep, but the twinkling multitudes had not yet awakened for the night. They could have been alone in the universe, were it not for the infrequent whoosh of another car or pickup rushing by. Every few minutes another few drops would trickle Nina's thighs. She would stick her hand beneath her skirt and touch it, to make sure it wasn't blood. Then she would try to be easy.

"Mama, do you remember the time the sheep went stone on me, and Uncle Tinker had to come look for me?"

Her mother smiled. "I bet your Uncle Tinker does too. He came back looking like he swallowed a bluebird. But he wouldn't say what had happened, you had fallen asleep, he said, you, who we almost had to tie down to get to sleep at all!"

She had first gone with the sheep when she was three or four, toddling beside her cousin Naomi, pestering her with questions, wanting to go home to the hogan long before it was time. When she was six Naomi was sent to school, and she had to take the herd alone. Before the sun was up she would be out with them, her puppy Graydog scampering at her side. The morning air was newly born, fresh as a bath and smelling of powder pine. The goats in the herd bobbed quickly in the cool, and the sheep followed dumbly, content to fatten on anything underneath.

It was in those first herding days that the valley became part of her, melting inside her like dreams. Beyond understanding she sensed the light painting the landscape, the sand underfoot and the mesas in the distance neither red nor brown nor gray, but whatever the light decided they should be. The valley's moods became her own, twisted pinons and junipers seeming storm-tossed in the quiet afternoon, delicate purple flowers clinging to life on barren rocks, afternoon wind spinning sand off mesa tops, trying to escape from itself and hide in the valley. Beauty and harshness mingled: rhythmic ripples of waterprints in sand where it sloped to a stream that filled up after a rain; sprawling hot endless dryness that stretched in the summer months as far as time; the hurtingness of the sun when it fell from straight overhead in perfect blue; scraggly patches of unripe corn struggling for healthy births in the dried-out earth; the great rock people towering proud out of the sand, seeming to circle her as she walked the valley. All of it she would come to assume was the natural order, the way of the earth, to be found everywhere; except the rock people, who were her own special friends. Hundreds of horses high they grew, red or brown depending on the light, rocks whose mother was sand, changing their shapes, changing their moods, watching her or ignoring her, playing with her or silently scolding her: the Owl Man peering from the mesa, the rest growing up like trees from the valley floor:

30

the Yei Bechai dancers and the Totem Pole, the Three Weird Sisters walking together, Coffee Pot and Tea Pot, Agathlan guarding the entrance near the highway; dark shapes in a mythic landscape of the brain; most of the rock people hazy in the morning light; most of them sleeping in the heat of noon; but coming alive with orange fire as the sun began to set; then cooling to black looming forms against the evening sky, till they went away for the night; unless there was a moon, and they stayed to play. Monuments, the Anglos called them. They gave the valley its name.

The grown-ups believed in the Holy People, and she would listen carefully when Grandfather One Blue Eye would tell their tales. But the Holy People lived far away in the sky; she loved the rock people more; they were here, and could love her in return.

Perhaps, she decided, the rock people were children of the Holy, and went home for visits in the night.

She was glad they were back each day. Their presence was comforting as she walked alone with Graydog and the sheep, taking the herd east or west or north, depending on which her mother picked that day. Still, she needed to play during the long, lonely hours, and was alert to any fun that she could find. One day, herding east, she found a lovematch of bluebirds weaving twigs for a nest high up in the branches of a cedar. Each time she herded east after that she would sit still as a stone under the cedar, watching the bluebirds finish their nest, watching the mother on her eggs. One unexpected morning four small beaks were chirping in the nest. Mother and father spent the day flying a shuttle of bugs to the gaping mouths. She sat beneath the tree as the birds grew bigger; and learned to fly; and left to nests of their own, never to return.

Herding to the west, she often encountered a light brown jack-rabbit with one white ear and a constant look of surprise. The rabbits were still about in the early dawn, ending their day of night as the herd approached. Several mornings this White Ear caught her eye. One night she stole an ear of green corn from the hogan. The next dawn, when she saw White Ear, she threw the corn to him. He flapped away, but she sat patiently to watch. After the herd had passed, White Ear crept cautiously back. He sniffed at the corn, then pulled it into a bush and started to nibble. Each time the herd came west after that, White Ear was there, waiting for the corn she always brought. She made him come closer each time to grab the feast. He never came close enough to pet, never lost the startled look he seemed to be born with. But she was content to watch. She wondered sometimes why other rabbits didn't try to steal the corn from him. White Ear was a bully or an outcast. She did not know which.

To the north, where the valley ended in a box canyon with a stream in it, she liked to sit in a high curving wind-hollow carved by the centuries out of the rock, pretending she was one of the Holy People riding on a rainbow. One day she heard squeaking noises from a crevice in the rock. She peered in the dark slît, and saw a family of field mice holding a dance. They were frightened, and backed against the wall, too far in for her to touch. Another day, when she was eating a lunch of cornbread in the hollow, a mouse ran out to grab a crumb at her feet. When she didn't move, others came to nibble. Soon, like White Ear, the dancing mice learned to await her coming.

When she was not busy attending the bluebirds, or the rabbit, or the mice, she collected pretty colored rocks in a goatskin pouch. Or else she gathered twigs, and seated in the dirt under a tree built a corral, or a small adobe hogan. Each day she tried to think of new things to build. Anything to pass the lonely hours. If a light she-rain fell, she would prance in it, enjoying the wetness on her face, sometimes taking off her velvet blouse and hanging it under a leafy limb to keep it dry, delighting in the prickly cooldrops on her shoulders. If a storm was coming she would try to get the sheep home before it broke. Sometimes it swept in too quickly, and she was trapped in the valley in the menacing dark, crouched under her blanket, a pebble in the he-rain, getting wetter and wetter, shrinking smaller and smaller in fear as the lightning and thunder roared about, and even the brave rock people cried. Those times she liked least of all.

Mostly she passed the time playing with Graydog, wrestling with him and throwing sticks for him to fetch. He was part sheep dog, part unknown, with hair falling over his eyes like a teasing girl. She played rough with him, twisting her hands in the wool of his neck, slapping his sides, tossing him to the ground like a cowboy wrestling a steer at a rodeo, rubbing his belly as he lay on his back in trusting abandon, his paws folded double in the air. When she stopped, covered with dirt, he would raise his left paw, as if he wanted to shake hands, and claw lightly at her shoulder or her thigh, begging for more. The gesture tugged inside her. He usually got his way. He had learned early, after several slaps on the nose from her father, that he wasn't welcome in the hogan; that his place was near the corral with the other dogs. But alone out in the valley, she and her dog were equals in their love.

One day Naomi came home from school with papers covered with drawings. Instantly she was jealous, and wanted to make some herself. Naomi gave her paper and colored crayons, and she sat with her back against the hogan and drew pictures of trees and birds and clouds, and Graydog, and a hogan with smoke coming out. She showed them to her mother, who said they were very pretty, and to Uncle Tinker and his wife Maria, who said the same. Filled with a new excitement, she drew some more, and when her father came home in the pickup from Kayenta she ran and showed them to him.

"You made those?" he said.

She nodded, smiling proudly.

"Throw them away," he said. "It's not good to make things like that."

He limped brusquely by her, shoulder ducking and rising, stepping in holes that weren't there. Angrily she picked up a rock, and threw it at one of the orange dogs that was lounging under a tree. The rock fell harmlessly, but the dog slunk away.

The next day, after bringing in the sheep, she drew again, planning to put the drawings away before her father came. But her mind was on the paper, and she did not hear him limp up behind.

"I told you not to do that," he said, roughly. He reached forward with his hand. She pulled back, thinking he was going to hit her; something he had never done. Instead, he took her drawings, and the blank papers on the ground beside her, and the box of crayons. He limped around to the other side of the hogan, and threw it all into the cooking fire. She ran to the fire to get them out, but they caught quickly, and curled and burned, the box of crayons melting in a terrible wax rainbow.

"Only sand paintings for ceremonies are good," her father said. "Other drawings can put on spells, you want people to think you are a witch?"

She shook her head, first no, then yes, then no, not knowing what she meant. She appealed to her mother, who was kneading corn meal into dough. "People have different feelings about drawings," her mother said. "If it upsets your father, you better not do it anymore."

Stung by tears, she ran up the road; then slowed to a walk, and wiped her face with her sleeve, and went into the small hogan of Grandfather One Blue Eye. She found him as usual before the fire, squatting on his heels, his knees drawn up, his flat black hat sitting squarely on his head, tilted neither forward nor backward; holding a cigarette he made himself between his thumb and forefinger, his eyes somewhere far away between the smoke and the leaping flames. He was not her real grandfather but her mother's mother's father, who had outlived his own. He sat most of the day in the hogan, except when he walked with difficulty down the road to share their meals, past the weed-grown hogan where his wife had died of the TB long ago, and another beside it where his daughter and her husband splattered by a tractor-trailer on a rainy night never had returned, leaving him to raise his daughter's daughter. His face was lined like turkey feet in the sand, and when she asked him questions he would stare into the fire for many minutes, and then his words

34

would come like frozen poems, sometimes confusing but always clinging to her brain.

She sat beside him, cross-legged, in the dirt, not speaking. After a time he turned, and placed his gnarled hand on her knee. A small smile scattered the turkey feet.

"My father won't let me draw pictures," she said.

The old man took his hand from her knee, and puffed on his smoke, and stared into the fire. She looked where he was looking, and saw only logs.

"The breath of life enters the child at birth," the old man said. "The child knows what is best for the child."

"Then it's okay for me to draw?"

But the old man hadn't finished. "Wisdom and knowledge come with years," he said. "The young must listen to the years."

She waited for more. Waited for him to say which was right. The old man remained silent.

"Grandpa, I don't understand."

He took her small hand in his leathery paw. He stared again into the fire.

"When Monster Slayer had killed the great monsters," he said, speaking slowly, choosing each word, "he traveled the world in search of other evils. He found a hogan filled with ugly creatures, that had sore eyes, and mucus running from their noses. Their names were Old Age, Poverty, Cold, Hunger, Sleep. Monster Slayer wanted to kill them. But they spoke gently, and in their gentleness he could not kill. When he got home, his mother Changing Woman explained: 'These you could not kill, because they meet halfway between good and bad. Poverty and Hunger live somewhere between that which gives pleasure and that which gives pain. That is why they should not be destroyed.' That is what Changing Woman said. That is why we have these things today."

The old man fell silent. He placed his arms on his knees, showing that he was finished. She stood, and touched his shoulder, and walked into the brightness outside.

Slowly she walked toward home. She did not know what the story meant. But she felt a richness inside, as if she had eaten roast mutton. The way she always felt after hearing her grandfather speak.

*****

The next day, and the day after, out with the sheep, she tried to build things, with twigs, and stones, and mud; but kicked them down in frustration. She wanted to draw; to make pretty things; what could be wrong in that? There was no answer she could think of, except that her father was mean. She hugged the warm neck of Graydog and sulked.

A few days later, as she moved out of the hogan to take the sheep, she saw a brown paper bag on the floor inside the entrance, left over from the groceries brought back from Kayenta by her mother. Usually the bags were burned, but this one had escaped. Quietly she folded the bag, and stuffed it inside her skirt. Then she saw a pencil lying in the dirt. She picked it up, and hurried to the corral. All the way out through the valley her spirits were high. They were going east, and when they reached the grazing place she sat under the bluebird tree, and carefully tore the paper bag into four uneven squares. She allowed herself one square to draw on each day.

The following week, when her mother returned from shopping, she asked if she could burn the bags. It was rare for her to volunteer for work, but her mother said okay. After that it was her regular job. She never brought home the drawings she did, but hid them in the hollow of a tree in the valley, wrapped in a piece of plastic she had found in the storage hogan.

Sometimes shopping wasn't needed for many days, or sacks of meal and flour were brought in cardboard boxes. Then she would have no paper left.

36

One such day, herding to the north, she was pacing in the cool hollow in the canyon wall, bored and kicking at the dirt, when she found a dark red rock of the kind she used to collect. She picked up the rock, and scratched it along the wall. It made a clear, bright mark. Excited, she made more marks, and found she could draw without trouble on the hard gray walls. The sun was getting high, and she left to bring home the sheep, but the next time she herded north she brought her goatskin pouch of colored rocks, and stuffed it into a crevice not far from the mice. Each time she herded north after that she drew on the walls, first across the middle, then low down, kneeling till the skin on her knees was raw, then as high as she could reach by standing on her toes, then even higher, by dragging a piece of dead log up into the hollow and standing on that. At first she drew the things around her: the rock people, the sheep, the hogans, Graydog, her mother and father and little brother Johnny, the baby Alita, Uncle Tinker and his wife Maria, her cousin Naomi, Naomi's brothers and sisters, Grandfather One Blue Eye. When she finished those, she thought of the stories Grandfather One Blue Eye used to tell at night around the fire. She drew First Man and First Woman, Corn Boy and Corn Girl, Changing Woman meeting up with Sun, her twin sons Monster Slayer and Child-of-the-Water. Little by little the curving wall of the hollow was covered with her drawings; like the fading pictures left by the Ancient Ones.

Adrift in her drawing one day, a traveler in a dream, she forgot the climb of the sun across the blue silk ladder. The hollow was shade, and only when she stepped into the blazing did she remember the herd. They should have been back in the cool of the pens an hour. She hurried to the sheep, but frozen in the heat, their ankles hard adobe, they wouldn't move. She yelled and waved, shoved their stubborn flanks, pulled at the staring woolly stone unyielding heads. Not a foreleg wavered. They would stay where they were till the sun dropped softer in the sky.

With nothing to do but wait, she returned to the hollow, and the thin red enchantment of her lines. She still was drawing when a horse's hooves she could have heard for minutes had she been listening came to a stop at the bottom of the slope, and were replaced by the footsteps of a man coming scrabbling up. She dropped her rocks and ran to the edge, just as Uncle Tinker rose to meet her.

"What happened, daughter?" he said, sternly. "Why are the sheep still out?"

She looked at the ground, ashamed; knowing there wasn't an answer. She did not like it when Uncle Tinker yelled at her.

"They just won't move," she said.

"Of course not, with the sun so high. Why didn't you bring them back in time?"

She stared silently at the ground. Water was rising in her eyes like a river at a dam. Tinker, blowing breath in exasperation, paced the hollow, till his head came up and his eyes saw the drawings that crawled over most of the wall. He looked at them for a time, saying nothing.

She pulled in her limbs and made herself small, bracing for the storm. Tinker came near and kneeled beside her, and put his arm around her waist. Instead of yelling, he hugged her to him, shaking his head. "Child, what shall we do with you?" he said.

She shrugged. Tinker with a large calloused hand brushed back hair that had fallen over her eye. "I don't suppose we ought to tell your father," he said.

Shyly hoping, she shook her head.

"I'll make you a deal," Tinker said. "We won't say nothing to nobody. But you have to promise me you'll take good care of the sheep, every day. If you do, you'll get a lamb all for your own in the spring."

She put her thin arms around his neck, beneath his cowboy hat. Their faces, he kneeling, she standing, were level, inches apart. "Does that mean I can't draw no more?" she said.

"I don't care what you do. So long as you don't forget the sheep."

She hugged him, pressing her small face into his shoulder, squeezing his neck. "I promise," she said.

Tinker patted her behind, and stood and stretched his muscles, and looked up at the sun still eyeing harshly. "Sheep won't move for an hour yet," he said. He moved back into the hollow and eased himself onto the dirt, his head propping on a boulder, his hat sloping forward over his face. His voice came muffled from underneath the hat. "Daughter, you think you have room on that wall for a picture of your Uncle Tinker sleeping?"

When they got back, Tinker told her mother she had fallen asleep under a tree. Her mother looked at his face, and at hers, and knew he was lying; and said nothing.

*****

Weeks passed. Cold followed the pinon nuts into the autumn valley. The sun, having business elsewhere, stayed for a shorter time each day. The pictures in the hollow remained a secret, hers and Tinker's, warmed by private winks. Until, one morning, the sun did not come at all, but sent low gray clouds to brood over a thick wet sheepskin that had covered the valley in the night. The first deep snow of winter. School was canceled, and all other work. Everyone would go with the herd, to stamp away the snow so the sheep could eat.

Her mother picked north. In the box canyon there might be clear patches where the slanting snow didn't reach. Rabbits watched their passing. An eagle drifted overhead, not yet hungry for rabbit lunch.

In the canyon, clear patches poked at the base of the walls, like bald spots on Anglos. But the broad expanse was covered. The family spread out and set to work, moving across the snow like insects stripping a field, kicking and stamping, shaking bushes, clearing the snow so the sheep could get at the blue-gray grass and brush. The sheep milled among them, infants at the breast, accepting the help without thanks.

After a time, snow fell again, first softly, like feathers, then harder, like salt. Her mother saw a hollow up in the wall, where they could wait. She called the children, and started up the slope. Only Tinker and her father stayed below with the sheep.

A gust of wind blew through her, making her shiver. There was nothing she could do.

The children clambered in first, and scattered, chasing mice, who had left the walls in hopes she was bringing bread. Then her mother reached the hollow, and stopped. She stared, eyes squinting, at the drawings on the wall.

Her heart was shaking inside her. She half wanted to say she was sorry. But didn't. She stood instead half breathing, half frightened, as her mother's eyes roamed across the pictures.

At last her mother spoke. "All this from a pencil, and paper bags?"

Confused, she did not know what to think. Then, like dawn, she understood. She ran to her mother and hugged her waist, and took her hand, tears replacing the snow that clung to her lashes.

Below, the sleet had sharpened to needle points. Her father waved to Tinker that he was going up. Tinker, frantic, shouted taunts, challenging the manhood of he-who-fears-the-snow. Her father answered in kind, questioning the brains of he-who-stays-in-the-rain. He continued limping toward the slope, stepping in holes beneath the snow, holes that weren't there. Tinker, unable to stop him, followed behind.

Dragging his lame leg, her father climbed with caution through the wet. His breath was short as he stumbled into the hollow, and leaned on a boulder to rest. His head was down for a time; then came up and saw the pictures. His eyes narrowed, dark and angry; swept to her; to the wall; and back. She saw herself running, blinded by hot tears, down the snow-covered rocks, through the valley, running till her legs grew short and the falling snow covered her completely, hid her from the world under a soft white blanket of forever, nothing but the whimpering of Graydog left to mark the spot. Instead, in terror, she squeezed her mother's hand.

Her father was about to speak, to explode in thick black anger. Her mother cut him off. "Now now," she said. "Later we'll talk."

Bottled rage mottled her father's face. His eyes black as burned wood were smoking behind painted breath. But the knife in her mother's voice gave him pause. Her eyes never moved from his. Flames crackled where the two glares met. Finally he spun away. He pushed past Tinker, who had just climbed into the hollow, and started down the slope in the spitting sleet.

Crying, she pushed her face into her mother's breast. They moved to the edge of the hollow, and saw the dark form descend the slope. One hand holding her mother, she took Tinker's hand with the other. Together in silence they watched the dwindling figure skirt the huddled sheep and struggle lamely across the quilted canyon, in the rough direction of home; till he was gone on the horizon. Then her mother, eyes on the empty distance, said: "You'll stay at Tinker's tonight."

Fear filled her bones as never before. Ravens of doom nested inside her, mourners at the childish idea her mother could set things right. The driving sleet sputtered, and turned to wintry wind. The family trooped the snowy slope and stamped again through the bottom, clearing hints of withered grass for the sheep. The bleak gray underbelly of sky hung low, the squeamish sun not wishing to be a witness. Still the ravens drifted in her head; gluttons awaiting a feast.

In early twilight they started home. The milling herd trampled lonely footprints that scarred the snow-white valley: footprints of her father. The left prints clear. The right prints blurred by his swinging leg.

When they neared the hogans she and Johnny stayed with Tinker's brood. Her mother continued toward home, two hundred yards away, the baby Alita on her back in a cradleboard, like eyes in the back of her head.

The others went inside to warm by the fire. Frightened, she stayed near the door, waiting, listening. At first there was nothing to hear but the wind's coyote noises in the trees; and the barking of hungry dogs at the corral. Then from afar came people voices, muffled by mud and snow, hard to hear but loud, then louder still, not words but nasty angry sounds exploding, hacking, hating through the gray, blasting and shaping like hammers on rock; her mother and father screaming eye to eye, while fear and the ravens laughed.

She hugged the hogan wall, fingernails scratching mud. The searing sounds grew louder, tearing into her body, wincing her runny eyes, twisting the croaking ravens to throbbing points of pain. She wanted to cry out, to scream, anything to make them stop, to leave her free between. Then sudden as a cliff, as if some holy one were listening, they stopped. The voices drowned in the night; leaving a nameless calm.

In the failing light she saw a stirring near the hogan. Her father was coming out. His rifle was in his hand.

"Papa's got his gun!" she said.

Tinker came up behind her. They watched in silence as he swung his leg through the snowy clearing, his features and his purposes obscure. From near the corral one of the dogs came scampering, playfully. In a frozen twinkling her father raised the rifle to his cheek, and squeezed an orange blast into the evening. The dog leaped distorted in the air, yelping from some shrill primeval pain. It fell to the snow, jumped again, twisting violently, trying to shake loose the hot lead fleas inside it; and fell in a whimpering heap.

Caught in a fearful pause, the dead space of a sneeze, the pregnant interlude between lightning and thunder, absorbing, she did not react. Then she screamed a scream to split the canyon walls.

"GRAYDOG!"

She stumbled forward, crashing through snow and tears. In three quick steps Tinker caught her shoulders, and held them tight. Her father, oblivious, still held his rifle at his cheek. Orange blasts continued, a second shot, a third, a fourth, a fifth, exploding the carcass of the whimpering beast, tearing flesh from bone as calmly as a butcher, till the whimpering, shuddering stopped, and nothing remained but splintered blood and hair. Then he lowered his rifle, and turned, his back to the unseen witnesses, and crossed the clearing to the storage hogan, and disappeared inside.

Screaming, she writhed and twisted in Tinker's hands, unable to free herself. He half led, half dragged her into the hogan, past the other children, who had crowded the entranceway at the sound of the shots. Against the far wall in a shadow away from the fire he pulled her onto a sheepskin, and held her there, till her screams had ebbed to muted sobs, like a fish on a line losing strength.

"Graydog " she said through sobs and swallows of tears. "My father. . .killed Graydog."

Tinker rubbed her back, calming her. When he thought she could listen he wiped her tears with his shirt, and took her hands in his.

"I want you to listen, child," he said. "Listen carefully. It's pretty dark out there. I don't know if that was your dog or not. Could be it was; I'm not saying no. But I couldn't tell. And your father couldn't either, your father was angry, child. A man has to be awful angry to shoot a dog. He was so angry he was going to shoot the first animal he saw. Maybe that was Graydog out there, maybe it wasn't. But if it was it wasn't on purpose, your father didn't want to hurt you, no more than I want to hurt you. Always remember that. He was just shooting off his anger, at the first thing that got in his way."

43

"It was Graydog," she said. "I know it was."

Tinker stared across into the fire. "I have seen men wild before," he said. "It is best to stay inside until the morning. But if you want, we can go and see."

She nodded, pressing her fists into her eyes. Together they walked outside. It was dark now, and colder. A thin crunch was forming on the snow, lending a starry echo to their steps. They were almost on top of the bloody heap before they saw it.

They looked down in darkness. The jumbled mass could have been any of the half-dozen dogs that hung near the corral; or even a stray that had wandered by.

"It's Graydog," she said.

She kneeled in the snow, her thin hand reaching to pet the dog. There was no place to touch that wasn't ripped. She pitched onto her stomach in the cold, and buried her face in her arm. Her other arm was stretched beside her, her tight fist squeezing warm blood.

She heard Tinker walk to the corral, where the other dogs greeted his coming with showers of yelps. He cursed them for not being dead. He found a shovel and walked back, and scooped the raw remains, straining under the weight, and carried the carcass away into the trees.

When his boots crunched back to the red hole in the snow, she hadn't moved. She lay amid sniffles and tears on a mattress of frost. He carried her to the hogan, and placed her on a sheepskin near the fire.

*****

Her muscles ached from the steel side of the truck. She shifted her weight, and rubbed her cheek in the comforting nub of the blanket. She remembered telling Michael of the killing. The concern in his face. Of how the next morning her tears had risen like dawn, and she had run and pressed

44

her face in her mother's skirt, and had been excused from herding that day, and rode Dawn Pony out through the far end of the valley, further than she had ever been, rode him fast till he was tired, then climbed down and walked beside him, walked till her feet hurt and then kept walking making them hurt even more, learning that the pain in her feet took away the tears from her eyes and the stone from her heart. Michael asked if her father ever said he was sorry. She said no, for two days he slept in the storage hogan, and then he came back, as if nothing had happened. Graydog was never mentioned again. But from that day on he let her draw.

Ever since then she had had a strange feeling, she said. As if her father was afraid she was a witch.

"Since you were nine years old?" Michael said.

"Eight."

They were sitting in his office, evening beginning to fall beyond the window, Michael smoking from a crumpled pack of cigarettes on his desk, always crumpled, like his always rumpled hair. The end glowed bright when he puffed. A nurse in white sneakers that squeaked came into the office and placed a folder on his desk, and glanced at the two of them talking (again!) and left wearing a fractured smile. Michael stood and walked slowly to the window, and watched the rush-hour headlights running on Cerrillos Road. As if he were searching for weighty words in the passing beams. But when he turned back what he said was, would she like to go have dinner with him, so they could talk some more. She said she would. Her heart beat a quicker drum. Her mouth got dry.

He took her to Pablo's, a Spanish kitchen she had heard of but never been to; a flourescent room in the barrio, with wooden booths that were hard on the seatbone, and tables of formica. As soon as they sat an old Spanish man came to the table. He had gray hair and white stubble on his face and a skull that seemed to be pushing through his dried-out skin. A dirty apron was tied around his waist, and a matching towel was slung over his shoulder. Michael

45

joked with him in Spanish, and introduced her. The old man smiled. A single gold tooth flickered in his skull.

"Pablo here has an arrangement with the hospital," Michael said. "Anybody we can't help, we send over for chile. If it doesn't kill 'em, it cures 'em. Right Pablo?"

The old man nodded. "You need medicine, you eat here, Miss. Don't take no-thing from this Doc."

Michael ordered for the two of them, enchiladas and tacos and Dr. Pepper, and sopaipillas. The chile was hot and burned her lips, but Michael liked it so much she did not complain, but sipped Dr. Pepper after every bite. The sopaipillas with honey were exquisite, like fry bread only far more delicate. Pablo made sopaipillas only on Tuesdays. Michael knew things like that.

While they ate they talked, of her work at school, of her new paintings, of his work at the hospital, the things he would like to change if he were in charge. He would never open his own office, he said, because medicine should be free, paid by the government. He couldn't take people's money for helping them. What he wished he could do he said was sell his house, which he didn't like, which they had bought only so his daughter would have friends to play with, and buy an old adobe in the country, with a workshop and maybe a barn with animals. To live closer to nature, instead of fighting it. His eyes took on a dreamy look when he said that; as if he didn't know if he ever would.

They ate chocolate cake for dessert, like pudding with fresh whipped cream on top, and she could still taste the sweetness an hour later, alone in her room in the dorm, the desk lamp glaring off her biology book, reading the same sentence over and over, words of pistils and stamens, dull words for pretty flowers, nothing registering, no matter how many times she read it. Wondering if she had said anything wrong. If he had noticed that she didn't like the chile. Afraid she had bored him, remembering how he had made her laugh, unable to think of anything smart that she had said. Wondering why he had asked her. Wondering if he would ask her again.

She stood and looked out the window, and lay down on the bed. She gazed at the patterns of plaster on the ceiling, and got undressed, and put her pajamas on. She sat again at the desk, because there was a test the next day, and read of pistils and stamens, the same sentence, twelve times over. Wondering.

He called the next night. She spoke in her pajamas, in the phone booth at the end of the hall in the noisy dormitory. He had had a good time at dinner, he said. Would she like to do it again? On Saturday night?

She would.

She stopped going to his office. They saw each other in the evenings, two or three times each week: for a hamburger and a movie, or just to talk, with her legs curled under her on the sofa in his living room, Michael in his rocking chair, smoking. Or both sitting cross-legged on a Navajo rug before a pinon fire, near a wall lined high with books. It was a large house, three bedrooms, with hints in corners here and there of a wife and child gone away.

He took her to meet his best friend, Buck, who had a pottery shop on Canyon Road that he shared with a leathersmith called Lobo. Buck was a stocky, jovial fellow with a small red beard and a twinkle in his pale blue eyes. He did not seem to judge her. She liked him a lot. Lobo was swarthy and smirking, with no home but a rumpled bed and a dirty refrigerator in an alcove at the back of the shop. He smelled of leather, and had a bell near his work bench that he rang with his foot whenever a pretty girl came into the shop. Strangers and tourists didn't know what it meant. He called it his poontang bell. She found him vaguely frightening.

Sometimes they took Buck along when they went to the movies. But mostly they preferred to be alone, sharing the still-warm embers of growing up. He told her of exotic things that grew in New York City, things from future centuries, railroads under the earth, buildings that scratched the sky, houses in which more people lived than in the whole town of Kayenta. The new words drifted from her head like plants in dictionaries, but there was caring in his voice, and it lent them a fragile beauty. She talked more, remembering things that had long since drifted away: a broken hobby horse that lay on its side near the hogan, getting grayer and more weatherworn each passing year, and no one throwing it away; the white-painted wooden bus stop facing east near the side of the road, a mile from the hogan, where she used to wait each morning for the bumpy yellow bus to take her to school in Kayenta; her first day at school, eating lunch at a stiff-backed table for the first time, instead of seated on the floor; her first teacher, Mrs. Blakeslee, yelling at her when she was drinking her milk and eating her apple and cookies, yelling at her to not keep her elbows on the table, not explaining why bother with a table if you couldn't lean on it; her second teacher, Mr. Porter, who pasted her drawings all over the walls of the schoolroom; another teacher lady, a substitute, who didn't last long, whose name she didn't remember, who thought that Indians smelled bad, and made them wash all the time, though her mother washed her hair each week with suds from yucca root; how she grew to like school in the higher grades, becoming what one teacher called "a good learner, which is unusual out here," though she often had trouble remembering the names of Anglo things; her last teacher at the Kayenta school, who she had for two grades, Miss Mabel Farmer, a black lady from Atlanta, Carolina, who liked her drawings so much that she bought her a special set of oil paints and turpentine and canvasboards, and stayed after school and taught her how to use them, and let her paint in the school-room after class while she was correcting papers, and then because the school bus was gone drove her in her own car out to the valley, or at least to the Holiday Inn where her mother would pick her up after shopping or Tinker when he finished showing Anglo tourists the valley; except when she felt like walking all the way, and the miles passed without her noticing because the

48

painting was still in her head; coming home from school and sitting quietly beside her mother in the middle of the corral, watching her mother feed a new lamb Carnation milk from a baby bottle because its mother had gone loco and wouldn't feed it; the cradleboard that had held her as a child, hanging from a peg in the hogan, still there after all these years, modeled on Changing Woman's sons', bottom board made from the earth, hood from a rainbow, footrests of sunbeams, loops of sheet lightning, lacings of zig-zag lightning.

The cradleboard reminded her of her baby brother Charlie; of the great wall of water. She told Michael what had happened.

*****

She was eleven years old, Johnny nine, Alita six, Terrence three. Her mother once more was big with child, eating pollen that had been sprinkled over a hummingbird, to keep the baby small. Her father, seeing her mother laboring, swore he would give up drink. For weeks he didn't touch a drop. He became the head of the hogan, ordering the children, making sure they helped their mother. Most of the work fell on her. She did it gladly. Taking orders from her father—proper orders—was better than his usual unconcern.

It must have been August, because it was the time of the sheep dipping, when the corn was growing high in the patch of green behind the hogan, and even lizards hid their heads in the shade. The outfit gathered the herds and drove them twelve miles across the mesas to the next valley under the stiff-burning sun, to the place of water and the dipping vat. Her mother wanted to come and help, but her father said no. She was too far along with the child. They argued, and in his new self her father won. Maria Begay stayed with her, in case the child came early.

The place of the dipping vat was alongside a quiet river that flowed in the center of a wash, amid stands of cottonwoods. The sheep were herded

49

into pens put up nearby. A brush shelter was built on a slope half a mile away, and two women from the outfit stayed in the shelter, to build a fire and slaughter a sheep and prepare a mutton feast for when the dipping was done.

The sheep bleated noisily in the pens. The smaller children played along the wash. She watched from outside the fence as Tinker and her father and other men from the outfit moved among the sheep with a doctor from the government. The doctor examined the sheep for disease, and stuck needles into their sides.

Then it was time for the dipping. She climbed to the back of a pickup and got an armload of tin can covers strung like beads on wires. She gave a wire to each of the children, and kept one herself. The children lined up outside the chute that led from the pen to the dipping vat.

Tinker opened the fence. The first sheep saw the opening and started moving through the chute. The others followed. When some sheep stopped and wouldn't move, the children started rattling the wires, banging them against the wooden rails, to keep the sheep nosing along.

The sheep moved till the leaders came to the edge, and saw that the chute ended above the vat. Then they stopped, and wouldn't budge; as if they sensed a butcher's knife instead of a simple bath. Women with long sticks poked them over the edge. Other women lined both sides of the vat, poking with sticks to keep the sheep moving, pushing their heads under the water with the sticks, so dirt and ticks would wash out. Twenty feet further the vat had a ramp and the sheep could climb out and stand in a sloping pen, so the water dripping from their wool could run back into the river.

The air was a clamor of hot sun and buzzing flies and shouting children banging tin wires, and the terror bleating of the sheep. Black clouds hung over the distant mesa, purple curtains of rain streaming down. The rain stayed over the mesa. No clouds came to ease the sun.

They had worked for hours and half the sheep were dipped when stubborn ones refused to enter the vat. They stayed at the end of the chute, no matter how much the children shouted and the women poked. Others flowed behind them, till the chute was clogged with twisted sheep, none of them able to move. Tinker and her father and two other men climbed in among the sheep and pulled them apart with their hands, pulling and shoving and wrestling. They picked up those at the end and threw them into the vat. The men's hands were scratched and bleeding when they climbed out of the chute. The children cheered as the sheep started moving again.

When the cheering stopped they saw a horse riding up far away. A woman was on the horse, yelling and waving her arms. It was one of the women cooking at the brush shelter. Nobody could hear what she was yelling, but a second later they didn't have to. Pouring over the slope like a vision from underground they saw a great wall of water, as high as her head. It was coming straight toward them.

"Flash flood! Run to the slopes! Run to the slopes!"

Men, women and children, shouting, running to the sides, out of the path of the water. Children screaming in the sudden excitement. She saw her father and Tinker wrestling fenceposts to get them down, so the sheep wouldn't be trapped; looking over their shoulders at the advancing flood. Alita and Terrence were at her side, crying.

"Run! Run!" she shouted, and shoved their backs. They wouldn't move.

The wall of water was roaring toward them like some ancient enemy. She saw Tinker and her father turn and run. She grabbed Terrence with one hand, Alita with the other. "Come, run," she said, and started running with them, toward the slope. She looked back once. A boy was still in the path of the water, trying to open more rails to free the sheep. At the same time she heard her father's hoarse voice.

"JOHNNY!"

The water crashed the pens with the boom of thunder. Posts were pulled from the ground and hurled to the surface. Sheep were lifted up and thrown forward. Rocks and sagebrush tumbled in the tide. Screams of animals in

51

gurgled bleating reached them as the outfit, standing huddled on the slope watched the homeless torrent assault the river, its gentle sister; work its violent will upon the river; lose its force in the space of a pulsing minute; flow away out of sight, in the wide banks of the wash.

The path it left was a hundred yards wide. The sand on both sides was dry. Half the pen was untouched, the sheep frightened but dry. The other half of the pen had been washed away. Sheep were scattered on the ground for hundreds of feet.

The outfit stood as one person, stunned. Then coming out of a trance she and Tinker and her father ran toward the dripping figure of Johnny, wrapped around one of the still-standing posts. She was sure he was dead. But he let go of the post and dropped to the ground as they approached. He had been caught by the edge of the flood. He had a big grin on his face.

"You okay?" she said.

He sat in the mud, looking up.

"I think my arm's broke."

Tinker and her father bent over to look.

"Why didn't you run?"

"I wanted to open the fence. I got it open, too. Another second I would've got away. The water threw me up against the post."

Tinker, examining the arm, said, "It's broke, all right."

"Doesn't it hurt?"

"Nah."

She ran her hand through Johnny's wet hair. She decided that she liked her kid brother. It was the first time she had thought that in words.

They took off Johnny's shirt, and hung it on a pole to dry. There were bruises on his skin, where rocks carried by the flood had hit his back. He said they didn't hurt. Tinker straightened his arm, and tied a piece of wood to it with cloth. Johnny clenched his teeth. He didn't cry. He had never cried since he was old enough to walk.

52

All around sheep hit by the wall of water were struggling to stand, water dripping. The outfit rounded them up and brought them back to the herd. The sun as hot as ever lifted kettles of smelly steam from off their backs. Three of the sheep were dead, drowned in the dipping vat when the wall of water washed over. Two others carried by the flood had broken legs from being dragged along. Tinker's brother Joseph took the pistol he carried in his waistband, and put it between their eyes, and pulled the trigger.

Some of the women wanted to put the dead sheep in the pickup and take them home for mutton. Grandfather One Blue Eye said no. He had come to the sheep dipping in a wagon, and was watching from under a tree along the slope.

"A flood is the same clan as lightning," he said.

Everyone knew you couldn't eat a sheep killed by lightning, or you would die. They left the dead sheep in the sun for the vultures and the wolves.

It was late the following afternoon when they got home. They told her mother and Maria about the flood.

"It could have been worse," Tinker said. "We could've lost half the sheep."

"It's good you weren't there," her father said, smoothing her mother's hair. "With the child, you couldn't run."

"Soon the child will be able to run himself," her mother said. "He tells me he wants to be born tonight."

Quickly the word spread through the outfit. Alice's child was coming. When the sheep were penned the people came on horses and in pickups, raising clouds of dust that swirled yellow in the slanting sun, and gathered outside the hogan.

She helped her father gather sand, and spread it in the center of the hogan. Maria who would help with the birth laid a sheepskin on the sand. When the pains came faster her mother kneeled on the sheepskin, and took off all her jewelry, and unfastened her hair and let it hang loose on her back. Quiet and nervous, she stood in a dark corner, watching. It was the first time she had not been sent away during birth. It was time she learned, Maria said.

A red sash was hung from the roof of the hogan over her mother's head. She would hold it and pull tight when the pains got worse.

The labor was slow. She could see sweat on her mother's forehead. Strands of hair caught in the sweat and stuck to her temples. Outside, to help with the labor, all the women of the outfit let down their hair. Her father pulled off his red headband. When the baby still didn't come, Johnny was sent running to untie all the horses. To free the baby to come out.

The pains came quicker. Maria rubbed pollen on her mother's bulging belly, round and pale in the dimness, a full moon on a clouded night. Her father kneeled behind, pressing for support. Maria kneeled alongside, waiting to receive the child.

Her mother grabbed the sash and pulled tight, till her knuckles turned white. Twists of pain tightened the muscles in her face. Drops of sweat fell from her mother's nose, and from her chin. Not a sound escaped her lips. Then the pain seemed to fall away, and a look of peace as deep as oceans settled on her face. Changing Woman herself could not have looked prettier when she gave birth to the children of the Sun.

The baby poked its head for the breath of life. It was ugly, and covered with blood. She thought some terrible mistake had been made. She thought the baby was dead.

Maria cut the cord. The baby cried.

Her mother lay back on the sheepskin, eyes closed. Maria bathed the baby, and wrapped it snugly in a blanket. It was a beautiful boy, she said. Her father took the bath water outside, and dumped it in a hole in the ground; so no one would touch it by mistake, and get a humpback.

She went outside. The relatives were laughing and joking. The flood already was forgotten. The dead sheep had been a punishment for something;

some violation of the natural order. The birth of a healthy child meant that order had been restored.

Her mother was praised by everyone for not crying out during the birth. The afterbirth was buried, to keep it away from witches. The cord was left to dry overnight. The next day her father buried it beneath the horse corral, so his new son would be a good rider, and own many horses. The baby was fed pollen for four days. On the fourth day her mother's brother Joseph named the child. He chose the name of his mother's grandfather, Charlie, who had lived to 93. That way the baby would have a ripe old age.

Her father set to work to make a cradle. No one had ever seen him so happy at the birth of a child. When the cradleboard was done he made it beautiful with turquoise and silver beads. He hung buckskin pouches from it, filled with pollen that had been shaken over the feathers of a nighthawk. This would make the child content during the day, and sleep soundly at night. She watched in joyous silence. It was as if a new, happy spirit had entered the hogan. Others rejoiced at the baby. She rejoiced at the father.

The new contentment sang in the hogan like bluebirds in a tree. She did not know what dream, what vision, what taking leave of witches, had caused him to change. She dared not question it, for fear of breaking the spell. Lying on her sheepskin at night, she mouthed words of thanks to Changing Woman, to the Holy People, even to the God of the whites. To whoever might be responsible. He still was not affectionate, still never touched her, but he was different: not drinking, not complaining. Once, when she brought her newest paintings home from school in the autumn, he even grunted his approval.

It was not to last. The winter that followed was long and hard. Snow fell almost every day. They worked all day to clear the brush for the sheep. For days at a time the snow on the dirt roads stopped even the pickups from getting through to Kayenta. They lived for day after day on soup and bread. The sheep grew thin and weak. Silent wolves attacked them in the pens. One week Tinker and her father took turns staying up all night, to sit huddled in the pen with a shotgun, keeping the wolves away. Another week the cold was as bad as anyone could remember. Each morning that week sheep were found dead, starved or frozen in the night.

Finally the weather broke. The sun burned bright in a clear blue sky, turning the snow to water, turning the roads to mud.

That week the baby Charlie took sick.

His face got red. His skin grew hot. He cried all the time, and wouldn't eat. A medicine man was sent for, and prescribed certain herbs. The baby grew calmer, but still didn't eat. He grew thin and quiet, where he used to be fat and happy. Her mother insisted they take him to the hospital at Window Rock.

Her mother and father took Charlie one morning in the pickup. They did not return till night. She ran to meet them, Tinker and Maria alongside. Her mother carrying the baby hugged Maria, and hurried into the hogan. She looked like she had been crying. Her father was dark and scowling, his face a bloody tomahawk.

"They told us the baby will die," he said. "He has the sickness they call TB, and something worse. The hospital is all filled up. They made us take him home. They said he will die wherever."

Tinker clasped her father to his breast. She hugged them both. Her father, in his grief, didn't seem to notice.

For two days the baby got worse. The second night her mother said the baby was going to die. She wrapped him in four blankets, and placed him on the ground outside. So he would not die in the hogan. So they would not have to move.

The night was February cold, with clouds hiding the stars. After ten minutes, her mother stood, and peered out. She could not leave the baby alone. She wrapped herself in blankets and lay beside him, on a sheepskin on the frozen earth.

Terrence and Alita went outside. Terrence, looking down, said, "Don't die, mama."

She took her brother and sister in, and stretched with them on a sheep-skin, a child's head in the curve of each of her arms, until they slept. Her mother remained outside, with the baby. In the morning, Charlie was dead.

*****

New snow fell all day in a playless world. The children lurked obscure in rounded corners. Faded images floated in her head, of the gray-haired wife of Grandfather One Blue Eye, dying in a hogan of childhood past; of men crashing the hogan wall; of the family moving here, further into the valley. The old hogan near the road was mostly hidden now by weeds growing through the roof and out the walls. The saying was that ghosts were tangled inside.

Dying was a trick the old played on the young. She didn't understand how Charlie learned it so quick.

When her mother was busy she used to feed Charlie his mush from a wooden spoon. She had been the first to see him smile, and showed the others. She had wondered for days what gift to give him, and settled finally on a blue clay horse she had made at school. He took it in his tiny fingers and smiled again, and pressed it to his face, and wouldn't let it go. After that he would never eat unless he was holding his blue clay horse. Seeing this, Grandfather One Blue Eye said Charlie's secret name, to be kept in the family and used only in ceremonies, should be Blue Horse.

One day, in a tantrum, twisting his head away from the spoon, Charlie threw the blue horse to the ground. The head broke off. Scolding, she showed the broken horse to Charlie. He took it and held it tight, and finished his food. He seemed to love the headless horse as much as before.

She saw it now, lying on the floor against the wall.

In the lightfalling snow her father was working near the storage hogan, nailing wood together; making a box. Lines showed near his eyes as he strained to make the corners perfect, bent like a silversmith over his work. She watched in silence; then walked to the brush, where her mother was preparing Charlie. She had taken off his clothes, and was washing his small body with water from a basin. When she was through she dressed him again; and wrapped him in a blanket.

Her father walked up, carrying the coffin in widespread arms, a hammer lying on the top. Johnny trailed behind, carrying a shovel. Nobody said a word. Nobody seemed to have spoken all the day. They did their parts as in a dance they had always known.

They walked to the slope of the mesa. Her father placed the wooden box on the ground. He was wearing rubber boots against the new snow, but he had forgotten to buckle them. The tops flapped loosely, and the insides were filling with white.

He took Charlie, a dead weight in a blanket now, and placed him carefully in the box. He stared for a time at the small face peeping motionless from the folds. The others waited. Her mind raced from the ground to the faraway mountains, leaping desperately toward the sky, held by invisible chains. The sharp whack of a hammer snapped her to earth.

"Wait!"

Her father paused, another hammer blow hanging in the air. They looked at her as if some foul word had burst, dirtying the ground all around. Quickly she groped in the pocket of her skirt, and pulled out the headless blue horse.

Her father, kneeling by the coffin, looked at her eyes. She sank to her knees beside him in the snow. He lifted the lid, the first nail sticking out the top. She started to place the horse in the coffin. But midway she changed direction, and handed it instead to him.

Her father took the headless horse and looked at it, and at her. She felt at once warm and stripped clean; as if he were seeing her for the first time. He

58

reached toward her with the hand that held the horse, and he rubbed the back of his hand, gently, again and again, against her cheek, his eyes not leaving hers. Then he leaned forward, and tucked the horse amid the folds of blanket in the coffin. Tears washed her face as the stutter of hammer blows nailed the coffin shut in harnessed anger.

They buried Charlie under a cedar on the slope. When they were done her mother led the way home, a handkerchief at her face. Johnny carried the shovel. The hammer dangled loosely from her hand, handle down, like a wooden extension of her arm. Fireglow burned her cheek where her father's hand had touched. He did not walk home with them. He stayed behind under the cedar, squatting alone beside the newly turned earth.

Dim dread shapes loomed in her path the rest of the day, mountain-slopes in mist, ready to loose from beautiful faces a deadly avalanche. The glow on her cheek insisted on good times coming; on a lost father reborn. The emptiness in her stomach said Charlie's death had buried the only hope.

In the evening, near the corral, she overheard her father talking with Tinker. Bitterness like a hoarse crow had returned to his voice. "This TB what killed Charlie, it's a white man's sickness," he said. "The kitcarsons brought it here. Now the white men don't catch it no more. Only The People catch it. Only The People die."

She heard him thrashing through the night. He had to go away, he told them. He would visit his mother's family, near Window Rock. He would return after a week. He put on his best jewelry, to impress his mother; and drove away.

Ten days passed. Her mother was unconcerned. Until early one afternoon amid the barking of the dogs a sleek maroon pickup churned the dust. It was her father's younger brother, Harry Yazzie, who worked at tribal headquarters in Window Rock. He was stopping by to visit, he said, on a business trip to Kayenta.

"Where's my husband?" her mother said.

Harry looked down, dropping his pretense. "Was he going to my mother's?"

Her mother nodded.

"He never came," Harry said. "Someone saw him yesterday in Gallup. Drinking his jewelry away."

Her mother rubbed a hand across her brow. Her heart sank lower in her chest, like the evening sun when it fell behind the cliff; saying a long dark night lay ahead, a long dark night when you cannot sleep, and morning refuses to come.

"It's not my place to get him," Harry said. "I thought I better come tell you. I'll drive you to Gallup if you want."

They were on the road in an hour. She sat in the front of the pickup, between Harry and her mother, the other children left with Maria Begay. The gleaming truck sped smoothly, minus the creaks and rattles of everyone else's.

"It was the baby that did it," Harry said.

The second sun shining from the hood hurt her eyes.

"He was really trying this time," her mother said. "I thought it was finished. He's a good man, deep down. But he's got this idea that he's bad, that there's evil living inside him. He drinks to make the feeling go away. When the baby was coming, he made up his mind to change. He worked so hard. He sang all the chants perfect. He sprinkled all the pollen. You should have seen him, picking a tree for the cradleboard. Making sure ten times that it was never struck by lightning. He never tied a knot. He didn't break pots. Nothing. All the omens were good. Then the baby got sick. There was no reason for that baby to die. He looked at the dead baby and he thought, it's his fault. There must be some evil inside him, for the chants not to work, for the pollen not to work. This evil he always worried about, it was coming true again. So he went to get drunk. He was ashamed to drink again in front of us, I suppose. So he went to Gallup."

60

"Mama, do you think the ghost of the wolf girl is still inside him?"

There was no response. All three kept their eyes ahead on the sunlit winter road rushing by underneath. Harry leaned forward, and switched on the radio. The loud rock music offered cover for their thoughts.

The station faded into static. She twisted the dial. The music was the same. Between the songs were commercials for businesses in Albuquerque, New Mexico. Used-car dealers. All-you-can-eat Mexican buffets. Hamburger places. Loan agencies. Hair dressers. Pet shops. A mortuary. ("Don't your loved ones deserve the best?") The happy used-car dealer again.

They passed a rodeo ground, empty in the cold afternoon. Beyond it, clusters of cinderblock homes, at once cozy and prisonlike. They braked down a steep swooping hill, past more houses, across railroad tracks; and waited at a red light at an intersection blocked with cars. Main Street, Gallup.

Harry dropped them at the west end of town. He would drive east, and walk back, asking after her father, looking for his battered green pickup. They would meet in an hour on the bench at the railroad station.

Tremulous, she looked about, holding her mother's hand. She had heard of Gallup: a place where evil dwelled; a white man's hell reserved for Indians. Whiskey and bodies burned all day in the streets. Rape and murder were sold at the corner store. They came in bottles. So she had heard.

It was a city like some she had seen on the television at her friend Annie's house in Kayenta. A rail yard with row after row of iron cars, round silver cars gleaming in the sun, for carrying oil to cities far away, her mother said. Great yellow engines marked "Santa Fe" She didn't know what it meant, but she liked the sound. Autos lining both sides of the street, filling the center, edging slowly in the traffic, more cars than she had ever seen; honking at people who crossed in front of them; the people turning and yelling back. On the sidewalk, people walking, others leaning against buildings, drinking beer from cans, drinking wine from bottles in paper bags.

Women in wide skirts and blankets, men wearing blue jeans, plaid shirts, old Army jackets. Navajos, like herself.

Her mother talked to a woman in the street. The woman shook her head. She watched children kicking empty cans in a vacant lot. At the back of the lot wooden shacks tilted, broken glass in the window frames. Underwear danced on ropes. A dog ran among the children, hopping on three legs, its front paw hanging limp, the bone sticking out. She remembered what her father said once: "Gallup is what happens when The People become white."

They moved down the street, toward the center of the town, past stores with western shirts in the window, past stores with cowboy boots in the window, past stores marked Old Pawn, with silver belts and turquoise bracelets and eardrops in glass cases. The smell of whiskey drifted out of bars, the blue-gray light of TV screens flickering inside. A man with no legs, his pants pinned up, leaned on crutches in an olive overcoat against the faded gray wall of a three-story hotel. The word Hotel, once painted red, was barely visible over the door.

Her mother disappeared into the lobby. She waited on the corner, pulling her blanket tighter around her shoulders. Across the narrow side street three young men were leaning against a wall, drinking beer. Their shouts burned her ears.

"Hey—Look at the fresh mutton."

"Right off the farm, sweet and pure."

"Like some corn, honey? Want to eat some corn?"

She hurried into the small, mote-filled lobby. A slashed leather couch claimed the center, a dying chair beside it. Broken butts dotted the floor beside an empty ash tray. The floor was made of hexagonal tiles, once white, now gray. The place smelled like the toilet at the gas station in Kayenta. A white-haired man with a round glass eye was behind a chest-high counter, talking to her mother.

She stared, fascinated. His glass eye never blinked, never closed.

62

They left the lobby and turned into the side street, past the three young men, who up close looked more like teenaged boys. The boys said nothing, but she could feel their eyeballs crawling under her skirt. She was on their land; they could do whatever they wanted. She felt her nipples tighten under her blouse.

The second block sloped up a hill. Halfway up another sign that once said Hotel hung from a rusty pipe above an alley. They turned into the narrow passageway, and stopped. A man was in the alley, urinating. They walked up the hill, and waited. When the man left the alley, they returned. A gray cat licking urine watched intently as they lifted their skirts to pass.

The alley opened into a square courtyard, already gray with evening in the afternoon. Four rows of windows towered on all sides, all of them blocked by faded black shades pulled all the way down behind grime-streaked glass. In one wall was an ochre door of peeling paint. Fresh red had been splashed across the ochre, spelling the word Hotel in dripping fire.

Together they started toward it. Halfway across she stopped, and grabbed her mother's arm. In a corner of the courtyard was a pile of garbage cans and yellow plastic bags. Sprawled across the top, in blue jeans and a plaid shirt too thin for winter chill, was a man: either sleeping, or passed out, or dead.

It was her father.

He didn't move a muscle when her mother raised his head. A dark mark slashed his cheek where his face had rested on the edge of an open can. Her mother shoved his legs toward the ground. They dangled motionless. Then slowly his lids pulled back, exposing the red and gray of dying ash.

"Let's go home," her mother said.

A look of concentration crossed her father's face. He peered at them, as if trying to remember who they were. With great effort he raised his legs to the adjacent can; and passed out again.

"He doesn't even recognize us," her mother said.

Horrified, she realized that he did.

63

The railroad station was three blocks away. She found Harry waiting beside the battered green pickup, which he had found at the other end of town. Four pink tickets were clutched in the broken wiper.

A shoulder under each armpit, her mother and Harry walked her father through the narrow alley, husband, brother, not helping, not resisting, muttering "got to do it... got to do it," his tongue as thick as lard. Half scrambling, half pushed, he tumbled noisily onto the tin floor of the pickup. He didn't move from where he landed.

Her mother nodded to Harry. They started back without him through the evening, her mother driving, her father shapeless in the back of the truck, like a sack of flour from the trading post; with small black bugs inside.

In the quick-falling dark she leaned her head on the cracked side window, and escaped into sleep. She dreamed of men eating ears of corn in front of girls with round glass eyes that couldn't close.

*****

Thumping, like a giant's frightened heartbeat, shook Tinker's pickup. The breeze rippled slower on Nina's face. Thumping merged with a clatter of hail underneath. Gravel from the side of the highway. The pickup stopped, the door slammed, sounding tinny in the night. Tinker was out in back, the harsh red of the brake light coloring his face.

"Son of a coyote!" he said.

The tailgate screeched in mortal protest as he pulled it down.

"Flat tire," he said. "Been meanin' to change it for weeks. That's what you get." Looking at Nina, "How you doing, girl?"

"Okay," Nina said.

She was leaking badly. The sudden thumping had shaken her. She envisioned the baby drying up, a seven-month lump of dead inside. Sweat froze her brow. She felt herself shaking, not with cold but with nerves. Speed was everything now. A starless nightworld of fear enveloped her as the truck stood motionless, a cripple by the road. A broken ambulance.

Her mother squeezed her shoulder, and slid feet-forward off the truck, to help with the tire. "Try not to move," she said. "We'll hurry."

Nina pressed fists into folds of skirt; pressed as tight as she could, trying to be a cork, trying to hold back the water; trying to hold back the end. Metal clanged underneath as Tinker wrestled the jack and started to pump. The truck floated up. Dizzy swirled her head. Visions of Michael spun inside her brain. Reaching out with stumps of arms to Michael.

As doctor, to help her?

As lover, to comfort her?

She didn't know. She was tormenting herself. Sweet Michael torture. It took her mind from the liquid staining her thighs. Pain was better than fear.

She thought of the growing-up stories Michael had told. The small boy beneath his confident air. She envisioned his house in the city of New York Bronx, six hogans high, made of yellow bricks turned brown by dirt that lived in the sky, with iron railings on the outside to climb down in case of a fire. There were steps inside to climb up to the third floor where Michael lived, and also an elevator like in the movies. She had never been in an elevator, not even in Santa Fe. The building was old and the elevator moved slowly, and Michael's favorite game when his mother and father were leaving the house in the elevator was to run down the steps and get to the bottom first, and be waiting in the street when his mother and father came out. He would laugh and say "I won!" and they would tell him to be careful and not run in the street in front of any cars while they were gone. Many cars passed in the street where Michael lived, every day. Even noisy green buses smelling of gas, with people inside reading newspapers.

Mostly he played with his friends on the sidewalk in front of the house, and in the dark sooty alleys between the houses, where coal was delivered in big black trucks to make the houses warm, and later oil in big green trucks.

65

Sometimes they played cops and robbers, shooting each other with guns made of fingers. Other times they played cowboys and Indians. They chose up sides. The losers would have to be the Indians. Sometimes the Indians would shoot the cowboys first, and the cowboys would clutch at their arms, bleeding from imaginary arrows. But the cowboys never got killed. They would always keep chasing the Indians through the brick alleys. The game wasn't over till all the Indians were dead.

The other way the game would stop was if the garbage lady came. The garbage lady was an old woman with a long pointed nose and gray hair tangled all in knots. She wore a black dress that was dirty and never hung straight, with a torn slip sticking out underneath, and black shoes broken in the back, and stockings made from dirty bandages. Her hands shook and her back was humped under a gray burlap sack she always carried. Metal garbage cans lined the streets in front of all the houses, and once each week or so the old woman would come hobbling up the street on swollen ankles, taking the top off every garbage can and poking around inside. When she found something she wanted she would reach into the garbage can and pull it out, and stick it in her sack. Then she would hobble on to the next garbage can. Michael never knew what it was that she took from the garbage cans. He was never close enough to see. He was too frightened to look. When some-one saw the garbage lady coming up the street, whatever game they were in the middle of, was ended. The cops and robbers or brave cowboys and Indians would run as fast as they could down the alleyways, and hide behind the buildings till she had passed. Michael ran the furthest of all, up the three flights of steps and into his house. Sometimes he even hid under the bed, tears flushing his cheeks. He had good reason. His mother had told him that if he ever did anything bad, the garbage lady would come and take him away.

To this day, Michael said, he sometimes still had nightmares about the garbage lady hobbling up to get him. He would wake up, his pajama tops wet with sweat, and stare into the darkness of the ceiling, wondering what it was that he had done bad.

Nina chewed her lip at the recollection, and smiled. She remembered the night he had talked of those things in his living room. He had cooked spaghetti for her, his favorite food when he was growing up, and his mind had drifted to childhood, to the little horror stories, and for the first time he had revealed his own fears, the dark uncertainties that dwelled inside his athlete's body, his calm doctor's manner. His face had seemed little-boy warm, and his eyes glowed with the dew of forgotten mornings, as if it had been a long time since he had talked that way to anyone. She had asked him why Anglos didn't have families anymore. He had thought a minute, and said, "We have television sets instead." He was trying to be funny. But he sounded sad.

Afterward, in the driveway, as he prepared to take her home, there had been a moment, when he held open the door of the jeep for her, when she edged past him, her hair touching his coat, that she thought he was about to put his hands on her shoulders, to kiss her. She hesitated. A second passed. She climbed onto the seat. He closed the door.

He drove her back all proper and polite. But some new tingling touch without a touch had passed between them. They knew each other knew it.

She smiled warm and bitter at the memory, and at the image of his garbage lady, so vivid in her head. Whites could laugh at Navajo families huddling together in a hogan, afraid of witches' noises in the night. But alone in their beds the whites had witches too.

There was only one difference. The whites who had witches were ashamed.

She wished her father were alive, so she could tell him that. It would have given him a laugh.

*****

Witches. Flat red witches' world.

She leaned her head on the gunmetal cold of the truck. She remembered the first day of blood. A few months after the ride to Gallup. Her mother had warned her. No matter. For a moment she fainted. She thought she had sliced herself there. Till she realized what it was.

The whole outfit was told. Nina had become a woman! They came to celebrate. She dressed in her best purple blouse, green skirt, conchas around her waist, favorite turquoise beads around her neck. Her hair black and shiny was tied with a special thong. For three chattering nights she stayed in the hogan with the women, grinding corn meal for her special cake. At dawn each day she left them, and raced toward the east, across the coral sand and the sleeping sage, till she was out of breath, and had to rest. The first three days, her brother Johnny and Naomi Begay raced with her, laughing, joking, careful not to get ahead of her, or they would grow older first. In the afternoon each day she was molded by Naomi's mother Maria, who had not yet grown fat. She stretched face down on her mother's best blanket in front of the hogan, the men standing on one side, the women on the other. Maria kneeled beside her, carefully molding her hair, molding her body, as if her skin were wet clay not yet baked. So she would be shapely and beautiful, like Changing Woman.

The fourth night the ground corn was mixed into batter, and placed in the pit oven lined with husks. A fire was built on top, so the batter would bake. All night long, a Singer led songs and chants inside the hogan. Toward morning, while the others watched, her hair was washed with yucca root. As dawn broke she left them, to race toward the east, alone this time. When she returned, she would cut the cake, give the largest piece to the Singer, divide the rest among the relatives.

The turquoise necklace banged her chest as she ran. She pulled it off and held it in her hand. Sifting sand filled her moccasins. She took them off, left the moccasins and the necklace under a juniper, raced off barefoot through the dirt, feeling the crunching cold earth between her toes, the energy of the earth flowing upward through her legs and thighs, surging into her belly, flowing up through belly and hips and breasts. She threw her shoulders back and ran with her head high. A rock cut her foot. She hardly felt it, kept on running. Rabbits hid in bushes and peered at her passing. Mourning doves fluttered from pinons, wheeled in wide circles, settled down again. Her chest was pounding with effort. Still she ran, as fast as she could, hair and skirt billowing behind her, breaking invisible tapes, out of the world of childhood and drunken fathers, into the new blue freedom of being a woman, into a great rich house by the sea of life, carrying her paints, carrying her budding body to golden warriors yet unmet, shedding tight cocoons of sticky candy, jumping chasms of dry wash onto firmer ground, passing one by one the rock people, the monuments, leaving them behind, all of them smiling proud; like parents.

A pinon branch reaching out like a man's hand caught her dress. She stumbled and fell to the ground, breathless, the dress tearing free, and rolled over and over in the sand, laughing, laughing, trying to sing, her laughter breaking the words, sky earth sky earth revolving as she rolled down a sandy slope, pushing the earth to keep herself rolling down, exhilaration flapping like crazy birds in the air around her, the pungent smell of burning meat tickling her nostrils, burning meat smelling unlike mutton but rubber burned from a tire. She rolled to the bottom and looked at the newborn sky, waiting for the world to stop spinning. She sat up, fluffing her hair with her fingers to shake out the sand, grinning a nameless grin at the broad upslanting universe, for no reason she could say except the joyous brink of life upon which she stood; and saw, about ten yards away, at the foot of the sandy slope, a solitary hogan, with thin wisps of smoke coming out. The smoke was not rising from the smoke hole. It was twisting slowly out the door.

Her grin faded to a puzzled squint. She stood, absently brushing sand from her skirt, and started toward the hogan. As she got closer she could see a blanket on the roof; as if someone had thrown it there to cover the smoke hole. She heard no sound as she neared the doorway. She peered inside but saw only darkness folded about with smoke. A stench of burnt meat filled her nose. She covered her mouth with her hand, and stooped inside. There was no fire in the pit; only glowing embers breathing smoke.

The smoke filled the upper part of the hogan. She kneeled below it. As her eyes cut the dark, she saw two figures lying on their backs in the dirt.

She crept toward them, and saw by their clothes that one was a man, one was a woman. She crept further, and touched the woman's hand. It was wrinkled and gnarled, the hand of someone very old, wet and cold to the touch. She let it go, a coyote of dread beginning to prowl inside her. She felt she was crawling in a dream of no returning. She inched closer, trying to see the faces staring motionless at the roof. She could not make them out, till she leaned her own face close. Then she saw. Vomit surged from her chest into her throat. She twisted her face away and swallowed it.

There was no hair on the heads. There were no faces where faces should have been. Only charcoal blistered burns of flesh and hollow. As if the heads had been held face-down in the fire.

Legs of pudding carried her through the door, and flung her into the cool morning sand. She groped for freshets of air in the mocking bright. The gorge in her chest moved neither up nor down. Sour coated her tongue. She looked at the broad upslanting universe and didn't think she could make it to the top.

Halfway up she vomited. She felt better. She walked slowly home, forgetting moccasins and necklace under the juniper. She knew she was supposed to run; but didn't have the strength. She remembered when she was

70

little, falling down near the cooking fire, her small hand grabbing a blistering rock. She still could feel the stinging pain that didn't stop for hours. She thought what the pain must be like of a face pressed in a fire; and fell to her knees and vomited again.

When she came in sight of the hogans she saw the others waiting to greet her. When she got nearer she saw it wasn't so. They were all outside but all she could see was their backs.

They were standing near a dusty brown jeep. The jeep was marked Navajo Tribal Police. She was relieved. She could tell the police what she had seen.

Angry voices floated from the center. No one noticed as she came and watched. They were looking at the policeman, chiseled in his light brown uniform, flecks of gray in the hair below his cap, a boil on his neck, a pistol in a black leather pouch at his belt; and at her father, wearing blue jeans and a flannel shirt, red handkerchief tied as always across his forehead, shirt pulled tight across his beer-grown stomach. His face was flushed with sweat. She couldn't tell if he was drunk.

"If you weren't there," the officer was saying, "how come your horse's prints are there? The one with the broken hoof."

"Well, what if I was there?" her father said. "I was out lookin' for my dog. Any harm in that?"

"And when you were looking for your dog, did you see the people?"

"What people?"

"You know what people. Old Man Lives Alone. Old Woman Lives Alone."

Her father hesitated, thinking of his reply. She felt herself starting to shake. A distant scream was beginning to build inside her.

"Yeah, I saw them."

"What were they doing?"

"Nothin'. They was just sitting quiet by the fire."

71

"What did you do?"

"I asked if they saw my dog."

"What did they say?"

"They said they didn't."

"Then what?"

"Then I left."

"They were still alive when you left?"

A tremor moaned through the crowd, like morning thunder.

"Sure they was still alive. What are you talkin' about?"

"What I'm talkin' about is that before you left, you pushed them into the fire. You held their heads in the fire till they was dead."

The outfit gasped as one. She screamed, and broke toward her father, not knowing what she would do when she reached him. The policeman stepped between, grabbing her. Tinker appeared from the crowd, and pulled her back.

Her father was shouting, "I didn't do that! What kind of man do you think I am?"

"You didn't kill those people?"

"They was witches! They deserved to be killed. They was brother and sister, living like man and wife! They had a child once. Between brother and sister! They was witches. The girl was a wolf girl. They been puttin' spells on me ever since my daughter here was born."

"Then you did kill them."

"If someone kills witches, it's self-defense. Everyone knows that."

"That's not what I'm askin'. I'm asking if you killed them."

"I didn't burn nobody to death in no fire. Only a crazy would do that."

"Okay, you didn't burn them. First you shot them in the head. Then, when they was dead, you pushed them in the fire. So the ghosts wouldn't get you."

Her father deflated, like an empty bladder. His fight was gone. He wiped his face with his sleeve. When he spoke again his voice was quieter.

"Anyone was to kill witches that was putting spells on them, it would be self-defense. Everybody knows that. But it don't matter none to me. I was out there lookin' for my dog. The people said they hadn't seen him, so I went away. That's all I got to say."

The officer nodded; kept nodding, pursing his lips. He wrote in a small black notebook, then put the pencil away. He looked at the others, started to say something, to ask a question; thought better of it, knowing he would get no answers. He climbed into the jeep.

"Too bad there weren't no witnesses," he said, "so whoever killed those old people could be brought to justice."

"Who cares about witches anyway?" her father said, looking at the ground.

The policeman started the engine. The jeep leaped forward a few feet, and stopped, the officer's face just inches from her father.

"Listen to me," he said, loud enough for them all to hear. "Times are changing. There are more people about. There are laws. It's not like the old days. People got to be accounted for." He put the jeep in gear, then stuck his head out again. "You see you don't lose no dogs no more. Understand? Or I'll be back."

Before a reply the jeep crunched off through the sand. No one spoke as they watched it disappear across the valley, in the direction from which she had come.

Excitement's child was an aimless milling, a waiting for something more that wouldn't happen. Her cake was forgotten, till the Singer reminded them. When they dug it out it was too dried up to eat.

The next day daily routine reclaimed the valley: sheep, cattle, weaving, school. Her father was the same as before; sober some days, working at odd jobs; drunk some days, sleeping wherever he fell. The killings were soon forgotten.

Till two years later, when the dead people returned.

73

*****

Nina bent double, a cramp gripping her stomach. It lasted several seconds. Fresh sweat kissed her temples like dew. She called her mother, who got a handkerchief from Tinker fixing the flat. She pressed it under her dress. When she took it out a dark red spot stained the center.

She clenched her fists. "Mama, what can we do?" Her teeth biting her lip drew blood as she tried to hold back tears.

Her mother folded her blanket to form a pillow. "Lie back," she said. "Be as still as you can."

Nina eased herself down, the sides of the truck rising around her like a coffin. From below she heard Tinker's straining voice. "Be ready ...to go...in a minute." The sky was black above her, leaking a hundred pinpricks of white. She closed her eyes, but quickly opened them. She was afraid she would sleep; would lose control; and the baby with it. She imagined the pain of twigs beneath her eyelids, propping them open. As she used to imagine then, when the dead people came.

She was fourteen. She would stay in school after class every day, painting, alone in the empty room, the smell of turpentine a private infusion, a heady refraction of a sleeping power within; squinting to keep colors true as the yellow electric lights overhead took over from the easily bored sun. She painted from memory: the lobby of the hotel in Gallup, the man behind the counter with one glass eye staring out; the young men in army jackets drinking beer against the wall; a drunk asleep on a heap of garbage cans (his headband a fevered yellow, so it wouldn't be her father.) She painted from life in the valley: a tiny shepherdess herding sheep; a man with a rifle shooting at a wolf (or was it a dog?); the rock people in the evening sun, alive in the colors of fire; then catching fire, hot flames writhing. She did a series, Agathlan, Owl Man, Three Sisters, Totem Pole, every one of the rock people, dancing or burning in the flames.

74

"Why do you paint the rock people on fire?" her brother Johnny asked once. She was stuck for an answer. "That's how they look sometimes. I just start painting, and that's how they come out."

The teacher, Miss Mabel Farmer, hung the fire paintings in a row in the hallway of the school. The principal, Mr. Conroy, told the class: "These paintings by Nina Yazzie represent the Indian trapped in the American holocaust." She didn't know what he was talking about.

One day the principal told her that in a year or two he would try to get her a tribal scholarship, so she could study painting at the Institute of American Indian Arts, in Santa Fe. Twin birds, excitement and fear, fluttered inside her. Leave the valley, mother and father, sister and brothers? Go to the Anglo city of the great yellow engines? Paint for real? A knot of nervousness tightened in her head. Points of color began to stain the gray haze of the future. The valley became a cradleboard, safe and warm. Outside lurked danger beyond belief.

Sleep wouldn't come that night. Excitement prickled her blood like swarms of gnats. When at last she slept, the dead ones returned. Striped through the door of dimless memory they crept, noiseless silhouettes, undulating purple fire, two shapes bound together, chains of rotting children round their necks; straining in dark to see their faces, blackness rising like tall police, blocking her view; kissing with blackened lips that weren't there, kissing, harder, harder, on the lips; charcoal faces empty burned and hollow, coming closer, coming closer, laughing soundless laughs through silver teeth; holding a wolf before their eyes, wretched wolf grinding sharpened claws, clawing like a cat, coming for her eyes; eyes of glass that couldn't close; coming for her eyes . . .

She screamed.

She woke with engines racing in her chest. She gripped the sheepskin, motionless, staring vacant in the dark; not sure it had been a dream.

The others slept on.

She lay awake through the night, straining her eyelids; daring not close them, lest the dead return. The earth froze in its tracks. Morning wouldn't come.

The next night was the same, and the night after that. Striped through the door of dimless memory they crept, two shapes bound together, chains of rotting children round their necks; cats' claws coming for her eyes, eyes that couldn't close. Hour after hour she stared at the ceiling, till merciful dawn-light prospered under the door.

She stopped going to school. Stopped painting. Sleeping through days after sleepless nights. Stopped eating, soft flesh hardening, hungering for nourishment out of reach. Luster ran like rainwater from her eyes, leaving dried soulless cakes. Aimless in circles she wandered the valley, stumbling over splintered bones poking from the sand, of cattle long since devoured; eyeing maggot-hide rib cages of horses starved and bleached in the desert sun; found in their white skulls grinning teeth; horselaughs from beyond. Wondered idly how long it would be before she joined them. Before she joined little Charlie in the grave. Wondered, without caring.

In time the Trembler came from beyond the mesa. An old man with white hair, his face tracked with the crawl of eighty years. He sat facing her, in a trance, his body streaked with pollen, his spirits far away with the Holy People, his hands held out, still at first, then trembling; trembling violent, as if his fingers had eyes, to see what she had seen; as if they knew.

At length the Trembler spoke: the ghosts of dead Navajos had returned to trouble her, were trying to steal her spirit; the Female Shooting Evil Way must be sung, to rid her of the ghosts.

The Sing began the following week. She did as she was told, removed her blouse and moccasins, sat on a sheepskin outside the ceremonial hogan; clutching her elbows with her hands; naked to the waist. Tinker and Grandfather One Blue Eye built a fire inside. They dug a trench around the fire with an axe, and buried in it a hoop of wild rose. The Singer prepared a potion, lacing warm water with sprinkled herbs. Dishes filled with the potion were placed inside. Beside each dish a mound of earth was piled on a cloth.

The whole outfit stripped; the woman and girls to the waist, leaving only skirts; the men and boys till they wore only breechcloths. They filed inside and sat on the earth around the high- burning fire, the women to the north, the men to the south. Sweat glistened their skin as the hogan grew warmer.

At a nod from the Singer she dipped her hands into the potion, and rubbed the liquid on her shoulders, her arms, her breasts. Flecks of green herb clung to her pale moon skin. Her mother, sitting near her, washed her back. Across the fire she could see her father watching her, firelight dancing in his eyes. She felt vaguely ashamed of her nakedness; ashamed of the trouble she was causing.

The others washed themselves as she had done, adults and older children helping the young. When they were through they leaned forward together, to drink the remainder of the potion. They could not lift the dishes to their lips, or the evil might jump down their throats. Instead they leaned forward, rears in the air, and drank from the dishes like dogs.

When they had drunk deep the Singer moved among them, giving each a feather from an eagle. She stuck the feather in her mouth, deep into her throat, till it tickled, and choked, and gagged her, and she threw up into the mound of dirt. The others did the same, the whole outfit vomiting in the dirt in the flickering firelight, casting backward shadows on the walls. The sweating would clean the evil from the outside of their skins. Vomiting would clean it from the inside.

For a time they rested, catching their breaths. Then they twisted the ends of cloth together, forming bags that held the vomit and the dirt. They moved out in single file, and dumped the bags in a pit that had been dug to the north. When they returned to the hogan she sat before the Singer, and he sprinkled her with fragrant chanting lotion made from sweet-smelling herbs. He sprinkled each of them in turn, cleaning them, cooling them.

77

Three more mornings the ceremony was repeated. She moved through the days as through a slowly lifting cloud, perceiving some new goal shining beyond a distant hill. An obligation had settled on her, the obligation to get well. The whole outfit was taking part in the ceremonies, sweating, vomiting, for her; out of love. The Singer was expensive, he would take two sheep when he left, but no one would complain. The payment was necessary, to make her well. The support of the others forged a tighter bond between herself and the Singer. It was not in his power alone. She, too, must work to cure herself. Eyes fixed on the distant hill, she determined to climb it, to see what the future held. Slowly she felt the ebb of her strength beginning to reverse.

The last night the Singer sang till dawn, invoking the power of the Gods. Making sure the ghosts were gone, and would not return. Tired from the ceremonies, she slept. The black shapes did not come back. Not that day, or the next, or the next. She began to eat again, feasting on mutton stew. Flesh became flesh, and restored her spirit. She returned to school. A week later, she started painting again.

*****

Metal bumped beneath her, the bottom falling away with a jolt. The tailgate screeched up, crying painfully in the night. She felt her mother beside her, blotting the stars. Footsteps scraped the gravel.

"All set."

Tinker's voice floated over the top, cut by the harsh tin clank of the door. The cold truck shuddered as the sleeping engine woke.

"How much further?" Nina said.

Her mother peered forward into the dark. "Twenty minutes. Maybe fifteen."

She could hear the nerves in her mother's voice. The tight control was giving way, bending like a cedar in a storm. The coming of blood had scared her. Nina sensed it, and grew more frightened herself. She tugged her mother's sleeve.

"Come, mama."

Her mother wriggled closer, stretching on the bed of the truck, pulling her blanket tight. Side by side they clung, mother and daughter, arms encircling; comfort giving comfort; locking out the fear. Children like everyone in a world of ghosts and witches; the order of the universe ticking in the pale new life they both felt kicking in Nina's womb.

Stars rode swiftly overhead, canoes on a misty lake. The truck was hurtling now. Nina could sense Tinker's foot flat out, his hands squeezing hard on the wheel.

Another cramp clamped her stomach. She eased away, slowly, so her mother wouldn't be alarmed; revolved and faced the vibrating side of the truck; drew up her legs and pressed her hands hard between; pressing away the pain. Wrenching her mind to other things.

He was a senior guide her first day at school, showing five freshman girls around the campus. Green-smelling lawns of newcut grass. Whoosh-whoosh of spigots throwing water. A minor luxury of the Anglo world, one of many. Dormitories looming, Santa Fe adobe. Athletic fields out back. A sunken theater across an empty field, designed by a famous architect, Soleri. Rarely used. A hospital for Indians, across an asphalt parking lot. Serving the Pueblo tribes. Whom the People used to raid. Steady traffic on Cerrillos Road. Across it a hock shop with female manikin legs spread wide, upside down, above cases of Indian jewelry. No one knew why.

A sleek low building near the gate. "This is the gallery." He was a Sioux, tan and slim, from swimming and riding, she guessed. Like the Sioux in pictures from a hundred years ago.

Bright, striking sculpture filled flourescent rooms. A six-foot can of Coors, yellow, red and black, crushed in the middle. "Indian Kool-Aid," the typed notation said. She laughed. A plaster American flag, two tits pushing through, full Indian headdress on the tits. "Heritage," the notation said. The others gazed in awe. She smiled again.

"This is the crap they haul out between shows," Robert said. He was wearing cut-off jeans, a gray T-shirt that said IAIA in red letters on the chest. His hair was dark. "Hopefully, before long the work of you ladies will be hanging here. So we can put this junk in the storeroom where it belongs."

The sculpture was good. She liked it, wanted to say so. Her fear on the long bus ride from Flagstaff, fear of confronting the white world, was melting away in this place. A reservation within the city; a gathering of tribes. She could imagine without difficulty her own paintings hanging here. Not right away, of course.

She was honing on a beam of light. It fueled her courage.

"I think these sculptures are good. They say something. They're funny. Why do you say they're bad?"

The others stared, mild horror, an alien from another world, who didn't know her place. Except Robert. "Some people think art shouldn't be funny," he said.

He held open the sparkling glass door, for them to move outside. Lagging, she paused beside him in the doorway; following the beam to its source.

"They're yours, aren't they?"

Robert lost a battle with his smile. He waved her out.

He was 20 years old. He became her big brother: confessor when there was trouble with the staff; tutor when mathematics wouldn't sit in her brain; cheerleader when her paintings shed the reality of the reservation, evolved into starker symbols. Looking at the work around her, rugs, pottery, paintings, sleek fusions of modern techniques and traditional symbols, the

80

direction most students saw as the only one, she felt driven to go further; to excel in a different path. She repeated themes from Kayenta, but with a difference: dropping all reference to time and place; omitting what was strictly Indian; retaining images from her past that spoke with a universal tension. Graydog, no longer shot by an angry Indian, emerged ghostlike, frozen in deep space, the hollow sun having no melting effect. The hotel in Gallup became a prism of reds and blacks, dwelling place for an endless line of the drunk and the damned and the doomed. An eerie landscape had a black sky, the sun peering like a frightened child from a wind-hollow high in the rocks; imprisoned or hiding; the choice belonged to the viewer. Robert's sculptures were good, there was talk of a government showing in the East, but he worried about the humor, worried if it was art. Whereas she—he said—she could become the best the school had produced, if she worked at it. Robert told her often. He was proud, not jealous, of his adopted sister.

The semester flew by in his company. Spring came warm and early. She made sandwiches one Sunday, and they went for a drive in Robert's battered Ford, the right front fender missing, the right front wheel rolling black and open. To Nambe, where they ate sandwiches and drank beer in the hot sun and watched the spring run-off of snow from the mountains pouring twinkling icewater over the falls into the pool below. They stretched on the bank and stared eyes closed at the hot white blueness while the sun painted beaddrops on their faces. In three months the semester would be over. Robert would leave the school, to an Eastern college or whatever fate awaited. She wondered if she would have got through the year without him. She couldn't imagine it. "How about a swim?" Robert said.

"It must be cold in there."

"Be nice and refreshing."

Slim form blotting sun to a corona, he stripped with his back to her, and plunged, arclike, to the darkling; ripples caressing rocks. He swam lean and graceful, barely wrinkling the surface. Her first impression months before had been correct. He had grown up swimming lakes in the Black Hills.

He conquered the rock pool twice, plastered hair gleaming, and waved for her to come in. She was sitting near the edge, toying with pebbles, wiping sweat from her brow with the back of her arm, shielding the sun.

"Isn't it cold?"

"When I was little," calling out, breathless, bobbing, "they used to roll me in the snow. Toughens little boys up. This is nothing."

"They didn't toughen me."

"It's not bad. Really."

"I can't swim. We don't got lakes at Kayenta."

"Better yet. I'll teach you."

She hesitated, shyness overcoming. Wishing she had brought a suit. But the sweat was sticky and the beer had mellowed and the canyon was empty except for Robert. It was not likely anyone would come this early in the year. She stood and turning her back peeled off jeans and blouse and underwear. Stumbling and flopping, she splashed in, icewater screaming in the curly midnight warm between her legs. Moonbreasts not eye-catching in clothing were larger in the soft raw flesh than he must have expected from her trim body, slim waist, slender legs.

"It's freezing!"

"Keep moving. Get the circulation going."

"The air is freezing."

"Go where it's deeper."

"I'm afraid."

He swam toward her, and stood. The waterline lapped their armpits.

"Lie flat on my hands."

She did as she was told; a mathematics lesson. His palms supported her stomach.

"Now kick your feet."

She started kicking. He moved with her across the pond.

"See. It's easy, you're swimming."

She kept kicking, moving her arms.

"Now I'm gonna let go."

"NO!"

"Keep kicking. Keep paddling." His palms fell away.

"NO!"

She swallowed water. She kicked and splashed, terrified of going under; kicked but couldn't stay afloat; started to panic, flailing wildly.

Her feet touched the bottom. She stood, gasping. The water barely reached her waist.

"You bastard!"

He swam toward her. She pushed his head under the water. He jumped high in the air, like a dolphin, put his hands on her shoulders, pressed her down and under. She came up choking and splashing. He pinned her arms with his own. She shook her wet hair off her face. They were kissing, the cold air forgotten. Pulling apart, kissing again, chests touching, wet arms pressing wet backs.

She felt a fish nosing against her thigh. She touched it under the dappled water, held it with her fingers. Robert moaned, softly.

Soleri's empty theater became their place. Three or four evenings each week, in the pinking dusk, they would stroll across the dusty field to the sunken bowl of the theater, sit on the white stone steps, talk quietly. Then climb to the control room, where they had hidden a blanket behind the lighting board. The moon rising over the Sangre de Cristos slipped in through the turrets, filming erotic shadows on the stone wall behind. If they squinted out they could see the sweeping arcs of the proscenium smiling back with outsized concrete lips.

Petals dropping with graceful doom from a cut flower; one by one, till none remained. Semester ended for seniors a week before the rest. No worlds shattered. The end had been implicit in the beginning; had been present in the water that day in Nambe. Three sweet months, without complications; after which, if they wanted, they could write. A sweet affection, a tender preparation; for a golden warrior yet unmet. They said goodbye in the bus depot on Water Street. The depot smelled of oil and exhaust, and bacon frying at the lunch counter lined with green plastic seats that swiveled. A drunk was asleep on a bench in the late morning. A blond young man with pale blue eyes was banging his fist on a pinball machine that said TILT in red letters. The idling of the engine rattled off the walls. She had the crazy thought that this is what it sounded like inside a lion's mouth when the mouth was open and roaring.

They kissed on the cheek. She watched his shirt and face change color as he moved inside the bus behind dark green windows. She hadn't bled for two months. She didn't tell him. Her body might be mistaken; disruption at the nearness of home. If not, if there would be a baby, she would tell him then. Let him decide then what he wanted. For herself there would be no shame. She would not be the first.

The bus doors closed. Green fingers wrinkled a wave in a cloud of coughing exhaust. The bus churned like a groggy awakening. The roaring fell away. Above the sizzle of bacon the blond boy with blue eyes still was pounding the pinball machines, his fist turning raw and bloody below the sleeve of his army jacket.

*****

She had a railroad ticket to Flagstaff for Sunday morning. Tinker or her father would meet her there. Instead she got a ride to Tuba on Friday with Mrs. Carey of the dean's office, who was going to visit friends at Great Salt Lake. Mrs. Carey drove slowly and talked quickly. She tried to listen but her mind wandered, and she soon pretended she was asleep. Through split lashes she could see that Mrs. Carey enjoyed driving with a sleeping Indian in her car. It made her feel warm and protective. Earth mother to the redman. She would be in a good mood when she got to Great Salt Lake.

At Tuba, standing beside the highway with her suitcases, a roll of canvases wrapped with masking tape, she got a hitch to Kayenta with a middle-aged couple in a silver Cadillac. The man had thinning red hair. The woman's was cadmium orange. It was the first day of June. The tourist season had begun.

"We're from Dallas," the woman said. "Daddy here is in rifles. Sellin', not shootin'." She chuckled at her little joke. "Though he does like to hunt a bit, don't you, Daddy? A bit? Why he'll take a shot at anything that moves. Sometimes I think he'd like to take a shot at me. Wouldn't you, Daddy?"

Daddy had a red face and was perspiring, despite the cool hum of the air-conditioner in the sealed-up car.

"Just wait till we get to that motel," Daddy said. "I'll take a good shot at you."

The woman was twisted in her seat, so she could face both of them. "Now you hush that dirty talk. Why, she's only a child." She patted her hand. "Aren't you, child."

She smiled, but said nothing. Through the tinted blue windows, familiar mesas were approaching. Excitement began to build inside her.

"You Navajo children are so pretty," the woman said. She strung out the word pretty, "You are Navajo, aren't you? Of course you are." She twisted further in the seat. "Speaking of pretty, how do you like this necklace? Isn't it a beaut? Got it just this mornin', at that trading post over at Cameron. Near the Grand Canyon, you know? The man said it's fifty years old, pawned by a dead Indian. Blue Gem, he said it was. The best turquoise there is. How do you like it, honey?"

The turquoise was Kingman, dipped in blue plastic. The silver was new, aged with liver of sulphur.

"It's very nice."

"Do you think it's as old as he said it was?"

"The man at the trading post wouldn't lie."

"See that, Daddy? I told you it was real. Daddy says not to trust Indians. Businessmen, that is. You can't trust any businessmen, Indians or not, he says. I told him, that's silly. Everyone's friendly now. Isn't that right? Isn't it?"

"That's right," the man said. He sounded as if he hadn't been listening.

The woman pulled the squashblossom up to her chin, and squinted at it. "This'll knock Lurleen dead back home" she said. "Eight little bills. Be worth the look on her face."

"That's right," the man said again.

She decided that Lurleen was the blonde wife of Daddy's younger partner; and that Daddy was in the habit of taking shots at Lurleen in various motel rooms in Dallas. She smiled to herself. She had grown much in the past year.

The Cadillac glided off the highway at the green and yellow sign. Holiday Inn was sluggish in mid-afternoon. The gift shop was closed, the coffee shop was empty, few of the girls were around. Mr. Watkins himself was at the desk. He waved to her as she waited politely in the rear for the Asa Phil Bennetts of Dallas, Texas, to finish signing the register and waddle off to their room.

"Welcome home," Mr. Watkins said.

She noticed that his hair was beginning to gray. He had known the family since Tinker and Joseph helped build Holiday Inn the year she was born.

"You're a few days early, aren't you?"

"Got a ride," she said. She looked around again. "Where is everybody?"

"Squaw dance at Black Mesa," Mr. Watkins said. "Whole valley's up there, your folks, too. Be back tomorrow. Weren't expecting you till Sunday, I think, your pa's probably home tending the sheep, though." Squinting, he filed the registration card of the Asa Phil Bennetts in a drawer. "You can be real proud of your pa. Really turned over a new leaf while you been gone. Quit his drinkin', workin' hard as two men. Yessir. Always thought he was the best man in the valley, when he kept away from the bottle. Him and Tinker Begay. But here, I'm talkin' your ear off, when you want to be gettin' home."

She left her things in Mr. Watkins' office, except for a small suitcase she wanted to carry. A car and a pickup slowed to give her rides as she walked beside the highway, but she shook her head. The sand felt good under her worn tennis sneakers. Her muscles were tight from riding all day, and the warm sun eased them beneath her white cotton blouse, wet with sweat at the small of her back where it tucked into her jeans.

Between the sand and the sun and the hazy shapes waiting in the distance, happiness danced in her limbs, a vibrant stream coursed through her body. Coming home! The valley with the rock people waiting had always been a joy to return to, even after the shortest trips. Now, after nine months away, she breathed the crisp baked air, and felt a perfume lightening her head. She wanted to run all the way; might have, were it not for the suitcase. She threw her right hand in the air, coolness washing her armpit, and waved at the Giant Agathlan, guarding the entrance to the valley. In the hazy, dazzling distance, she would have sworn that Agathlan waved back.

A raven glided overhead, toward a date on a distant mesa. From far above came the faint drone of a jet, drawing parallel white lines across the sky, blazing white in the afternoon sun and straight as a perfect arrow. She had forgotten about the jets. In bustling Santa Fe she had never seen a plane. Here in the valley above the earth-and-wood hogans they passed two or three times an hour, pulling perfect tails to unknown horizons; Las Vegas Nevada, or Los Angeles San Francisco.

She cut across a scrub field to the dirt road, starting dogs barking near the hogans of the Bonnies. No horses or pickups were in sight. The Bonnies must also be at Black Mesa. A mile further along she set the suitcase down and sat on a rock to rest. The muscles were tightening in her thighs. Out of shape from soft living, she thought. The white man's burden.

She wished she had gotten home in time for the Squaw Dance. Hoped there would be another in the summer. Probably there would. Lately people liked to meet people more. The religious part hardly mattered. Like Anglos going to church.

Her mother had chosen her father at a Squaw Dance. Her mother's face always softened with misty, looking- back looks when she spoke of it. Not-So-Fast had been visiting clansmen in the next valley. Alice saw him at the dance, off by himself, watching the dancing from the shadows. He had black hair and black eyes, strong muscles in his arms, a red handkerchief tied across his forehead. She was 18, tired of the boys in the valley. She was intrigued by the shy, dark stranger.

Midway through the evening she summoned her courage to its full height, and asked the stranger to dance. He paid her a dime, and begged off. She asked him again. He paid her another dime. When she had fifty cents from him she began to giggle. "I'm gonna take all your money," she said. "You'd be better off dancing with me."

Reluctantly he let her take his hand, and lead him out. As they walked toward the music, she saw that he was limping.

"Fall from your horse?" she said.

He didn't smile. "I was born that way."

She flushed and felt sorry; wanted to crawl into a rabbit hole. She thought of giving back his money. But the feeling passed quickly. It will do him good, she decided. She led him to the dancing.

He was tight at first, but loosened quickly. The drums beat a rhythm for the future that seeped into their blood. They danced every dance. Afterward, in the shadows, shy again, he said: "I'm glad I ran out of dimes."

"Me too," she said.

The marriage was three months later. Not-So-Fast worked hard to keep the approval of One Blue Eye, building solid hogans, well-hewn corrals, herding, farming, hardly ever resting. For two years they were happy. Until...

The end of the story always jumped at her mother too quickly. She could never think of what words to use.

"Until his leg got worse."

"Until he shot the wolf girl." Until Nina was born.

*****

She picked up the suitcase and moved on. Anyway, he was better now. Her mother's letters had been filled with the miracle all winter. He had been working hard. He wasn't drinking. He still limped, of course, but if there was pain he was ignoring it. He and Tinker had built a new corral. He had fattened up some of the sheep, and traded them for a smart new pickup. He and Johnny were growing closer, teaching Terrence to hunt in the snow.

"I haven't been this contented in years," her mother wrote.

That was the letter that was smeared with what may have been tears.

She wished her mother would be home. But perhaps it was better this way. Perhaps they could sit together, and talk. She never realized, till she went to Santa Fe, how little chance there was to talk at home. You were out alone in the valley with the sheep. Or the whole family was together. Two people rarely talked, the way she and Robert talked. Partly she understood why. Everyone sharing the same hogan, the same cooking fire, living so close together, nobody wanted to fight. Because they would have to see each other again in the morning. If there was anything bothering them, it was better to say nothing than to fight.

"It's the same at home," Robert said. "Instead of talking, they drink."

She reached the top of the hill. The valley spread below her. In the distance, the rock people stood, kings, queens, castles; a mammoth chess board.

At the bottom of the slope, the hogans, the sheep in the pens, her father's horse munching brush under a tree. Late afternoon breeze shimmering the cottonwoods. The scene, muted browns, spare stands of green flecked with yellow, spoke of peace; far more than the brightly colored postcards in the slim wire racks at the Holiday Inn.

They would talk. She resolved it. Alone in the quiet, with no excuses, she might even find the courage for the one fearful overwhelming question. She wasn't sure; but she might.

She followed the twisting road down the slope. Dogs ran at her from near the corral, barking in challenge. Two that she knew, Midnight and Rusty, who sniffed at her and then quieted, tails wagging. They remembered. Two new ones that she didn't know, who lost interest when the others stopped barking; one trying to mount the other, without success.

"And what are your names?" she said. "I'll bet I know. You're Asa. And you're Lurleen."

She set the suitcase down and stood in front of the hogan, looking about. It was smaller than she remembered. An earthen mound compared to the two-story dorm in Santa Fe. Whereas the valley seemed to have gotten larger. A vast expanse of eternity, uncluttered by roads, cars, exhaust, gas stations, McDonald's, Kentucky Frieds, Burger Chefs, Hiltons, Sheratons, Dennys, drive-ins, billboards, junkyards, traffic lights, stop signs, crosswalks, bars, liquor stores, supermarkets, shopping centers. Untouched, from the time of the Holy People.

"Papa?"

There was no response. She entered the hogan, and put the suitcase down. The dog she had called Lurleen followed her in. The dog had pinscher blood, albino, with a scab of pink pigment in her nose, white skin and pink nose making her look at once mean and cowardly. She shooed her out.

The hogan, too, seemed unchanged from when she had left. Sheepskins, pots, bowls, sacks of sugar and flour high up; her mother's loom, a half-finished rug threaded through; her father's saddle; cradleboards no longer used; cold ashes in the pit. Outside, in the brush shelter, sun spotting the dirt through the leaves, there was an addition: a double bed, headboard of iron piping, mattress resting on real springs, quilted cover on top.

For Grandfather One Blue Eye? For her mother and father?

She walked to the corral, said hello to the sheep. A large crop of spring lambs were nuzzling underbellies, drawing milk. The tightness of the long day's journey fell away, leaving peace. And under the peace a tight quivering string, like a drawn bow. Something was wrong with the scene she was looking at. She couldn't decide what.

"Papa?"

There was no response. She walked to Tinker's hogan, but it was empty. He must be out in the valley, she decided. He would soon be back. He would not have gone far, with his bad leg, without his horse.

She returned to the hogan. Barking and growling echoed from within. The dog Lurleen had gone inside again. She took a broom from near the door, was about to shoo the dog. Then saw what the dog was growling at. In a dark corner of the hogan, like a nightmare waiting for sleep, coiled, head high, was a rattlesnake; defending itself against the dog; prepared to strike.

She stared. She could get a shovel, try to kill the snake. But didn't dare. It was forbidden to kill a snake. She watched the standoff: snarling, growling white dog, its teeth bared ready to leap back; arch snake, ready to lunge in self-defense.

"Out," she shouted at the dog. It didn't move. She slapped it with the broom, yelling. She hit it again, harder. The dog, whimpering, slouched out of the hogan, tail between its legs. She stood to the side, out of sight of the snake. Watched its diamond head relax onto its coils. Softly, she spoke, as if to another presence in the room. "Hello, papa. It's me, Nina. I hear you've been feeling better. I'm glad. I'm sure mother is, too." As she spoke she turned the broom slowly in her hands, holding it above the brush, the long handle protruding. "I thought we could talk. There's a question I've always wanted to ask. Just one."

The snake was limp, at rest. Gently she prodded the broom into the coils. She lifted the broom. The snake hung coiled on the end, a nest of hornets, tranquilized. Slowly, afraid of stumbling, she carried it outside; set it in the dirt ten feet behind the hogan. As she pulled back the broom the snake uncoiled, and slithered toward a patch of scrub. She dropped the broom and sat on the ground. She wiped sweat from her face with the back of her hand.

She turned, sensing her father standing behind her. No one was there. Just a cedar, whispering in the breeze; casting a tight shadow. She wondered why she was talking to herself—and realized what was wrong. The shadow of the tree was short. It was too early for the sheep to be back in the pens. They hadn't been out all day.

Fear filled her brain. The snake... her father...

It didn't make sense. The snake wouldn't still be around. And where would he have gone?

But the sheep...

She stood and ran, amid the sagebrush, looking; in the distance; at her feet; for apparitions she dared not find. Dislodging moths, nothing more. Fluttering from brush to brush, a hummingbird; a moth, surrounded by flames; stopping, finally; realizing that he could be anywhere; that search was futile.

She brushed a branch with her arm, and saw a butterfly that didn't blow away. She peered close. It was not fully there. Caterpillar cocoon glued tight to the branch, butterfly wings flapping frantic, a frenzy of disbelief; half-born. Born enough to terror at her nearness. Not born enough to escape. Suspended on the blade of a knife, between two self-images, prey to every passing bird or breeze. Defenseless to its softest inner core. Nature at the point of adolescence.

She wanted to stay and watch it born. Watch its first exploring flight in the world of blue. Would it carry with it memories of brown? Or would those be left behind, in the dried-out cocoon, a storage shed of the crawling unremembered?

The distant bark of a prairie dog pulled her, plummeting, over the precipice. Looking up toward the sound she caught sight of the low mound of the sweathouse. Forgotten. At its mouth a tangled heap of red and blue.

She ran. Wanting to trip and fall, and not move again till the others returned. She stumbled. Her legs in their own surviving rhythm kept running.

His pants. His shirt. His boots.

"Papa!"

Nothing.

The blanket flap was down, closing the entrance. She placed her face against it.

"Papa!"

Only silence.

She drew her breath, ducked inside. He was propped against the far wall, staring at her. She drew back, dropped the cloth against his nakedness.

"Papa, why didn't you answer me?"

Heartbeats. No cloud of steaming air had hit her face. Only sour sweat, and something else. She lifted the blanket again, and went inside. Passed her hand before his staring eyes. Grabbed his shoulder, shook him.

"Papa, it's me! Nina!"

She pulled back her hand. His body fell, sideways. It twisted, and lay, grotesque, in the dirt; like a lump of meat.

She jumped back. Moved forward to touch him. Stepped back again, biting her hand. His skin looked gray. His flesh hung loose, like a flat tire.

Ravens screeched and fluttered in her head. She wanted to flee, to run from the *chindi*. Wanted to hug him, was sorry he was dead, her father whom she loved. Was glad he was dead, bitter flesh who never was a father. Was sick with guilt at being glad that he was dead. Was not glad, wanted to cry at the waste of him; her father, to whom she wanted to speak; lump of flesh who couldn't see—talk—hear. Ravens flying madly in her head, not two but twenty-two; darkening the sky; twisting tangled worms. Father who had fathered her. And limped away.

She pressed her eyes with her fingers, rubbed her face, steadying herself against the sweathouse wall; against a world beginning to turn. Shooed the ravens. Cleared her brain. She had to do something. She had to get him out.

She swallowed at vomit rising, and touched his skin. She put her arms under his, and pulled, straining, trying to drag his body across the floor. Dead weight resisted, loose flesh holding tight to the sand. Muscles groaning she dragged him three feet toward the door; then collapsed against the wall, unable to move him again.

The cloth around his waist has twisted off. She stared for the first time at her true father. Ashamed. Unable to turn away. It was small and shriveled, and flecked with sand. Almost lost amid hairy balls.

She staggered outside, out of the heat and a foul smell brewing. Saw an image from her art books, the pyramids of Egypt, tombs of kings; sweathouses in the desert, when all was said and done. She leaned against the outer wall, breathing heavily. Waiting for tears. Tears that wouldn't come. Only anger came. A feeling that she had been robbed. That no one could pay her back.

She tried to calm herself. To organize. White men are better in the trappings of death. Mathematics of the coffin. Visiting hours at the mortuary. At death one must organize.

She couldn't wait till tomorrow, for the others to return. He must be buried by sundown. The natural order.

She would get Mr. Watkins.

She stood, shakily, and walked through hollow space to the storage hogan, to find an axe. To let him out. Forever. The door swinging open hit something glass. A large glass eye that never closed. She looked behind the door, and saw two pint whiskey bottles, empty. And six bottles of Coors, empty. She kneeled, and turned a bottle over. Drops fell.

She didn't understand. Her mother's letters. Mr. Watkins, only an hour before. He had stopped drinking.

She remembered the snake. The snake was innocent. She had heard of such accidents before. A sweatbath too soon after a drunk. The blood still filled with alcohol. It did something fatal. It stopped the heart.

Why!

She carried the axe to the sweathouse. Dogs sensing her mood, barking. Penned sheep bleating. Late afternoon clouds gliding over the valley.

She didn't look at him again. She stood on the north side of the sweathouse, and jabbed at the dried mud with the axe; swung the axe like a baseball bat; jabbed again, swung again, jabbing, swinging, tears still blocked, muscles finding their own angry rhythm: Why. Why. Why. Why. Why. Why. Why.

The axe crashed through the wall, splintering mud. His spirit was free to leave. To go where it would go. Keeping its secrets.

She lay against the wall, breathing. Looking inside herself for a pool of tears. Finding only desert; dried cakes; bleached bones worn smooth from rubbing against nothing. Her brain a blank canvas, waiting to receive an image. Infinite silence stretched before her, gray and cold. Children might dance about, and call her "mama;" paintings with a quick, hard intelligence might dance about, and call her "mama;" at the core, inside the necklaces, inside the throat, would always be a hollow, a vacuum question mark, impaling: I had a father, once... I think I had a father, once. . . She could throw herself in whorls of Anglo traffic, running in four directions to escape. Or wrap in the valley's cocoon, the rock people faithful guardians. Follow flights of rockets to the stars; or track a single ant across the desert. No matter. One day, her face battered with the marks of time, brittle bones brittle in her back, they would cart her off to a hospital, to get her out of sight; to stop her from offending; from smelling up; from forcing them to see themselves. A nurse with large breasts would smile a professional smile and say, "my, my, what brought you here? I hear they picked you up by the side of the road, eating beetles." Her croaking reply would be the same: I think I had a father, once...

Numbness. Numbness and blank. And deaf-mute knowledge, like a faithful horse stirring. There were rituals that must be kept.

*****

The Asa Phil Bennetts of Dallas, Texas, were picking postcards in the lobby. Wearing the same clothes. No good shots, apparently, having been given, nor received.

"Well hi there, Nancy!"

She forced a nod and a smile as she hurried by. The woman's words trailed as she turned a corridor: "They aren't very grateful, are they?"

Mr. Watkins took charge: calling the lumber yard, finding handymen with shovels and spades. He drove her in his Pontiac in the dusty cloud of the black pickup carrying the raw board coffin like a sheep to slaughter; nails that held it together protesting on the bumps.

"I can't understand it," he said. "He hasn't touched a drop in months. Just the other day I was saying to your mother, 'Mrs. Yazzie, what the Lord loves most is a sinner repentant. I think it's just wonderful about your husband. He sure is a new man.' Just the other day I was saying that. No, sir, he hasn't touched a drop in months. I can't understand it. Your mother is gonna be sore upset tomorrow, to hear he's been drinking again. That is. . ."

She picked a place under a cedar, at the edge of the slope, alongside little Charlie. Alongside Blue Horse. She watched it from afar. Deaf. Mute. A pantomime. Afterwards, Mr. Watkins said: "Come on back to town. We'll put you up at the Inn, till the others get back. You don't want to stay out here alone. Not at a time like this."

"This is where I belong," she said. "I have to stay with my sheep."

She was conscious of too much drama in the words. She had meant it as simple fact.

The Pontiac and the pickup disappeared past mounds of gray in a purple sunset. The hogan was growing dark. She carried logs from the woodpile and built a fire in the pit. The dog Lurleen sneaked in and curled up near the fire. She let it be.

She opened the light blue suitcase, and took out a change of clothes. Trying to keep busy. Trying not to think. She looked at the gifts she had brought home for the others. New jeans for all the children. A black bowl for her mother, from San Ildefonso. A bright red cotton shirt, with pearl-colored snaps, for her father.

Her jeans were soaked through. After the chopping of the sweathouse, during the burying, she had started to bleed. The first time in three months. She had not been with child after all. She peeled off the jeans and underwear, and dropped them in a heap. She wiped smears from her thighs, and pulled on fresh clothes. The dog idled near, sniffing the wet panties. She tied her sneakers, and reached down for the jeans, to spread them out to dry before the fire.

The dog saw the thing at the same instant she did. The dog was quicker. It darted its head, a fighter jabbing, and came up backing away, and trotted out the door. The thing was hanging from its teeth. Bloody and pulpy, like a smashed peach.

*****

She lay face up on a sheepskin, waiting for the nausea to pass. She dreamed of a wolf biting an eagle, the two of them locked together, teeth cutting deep into talon, the eagle clawing to be free.

It was dark when she awoke. The fire had died to embers. The air was a thick velvet silence. She stood, and went outside. Every star in the sky was shining. A welcome-home party. Enemies all.

She was hungry. And alone with a deeper hunger. She walked to where her father's horse was tied, and rubbed its head. It nuzzled its face against her cheek. The evening air was chill, but there wasn't any breeze. The only sound was hungry sheep, bleating.

A quarter moon drew outlines of sheepghosts as they stood immobile in the pen. Except for one spring lamb, who was jumping about, bleating loudly; pressing its face underneath a mother who kept turning and backing away. She climbed the fence, moved among them, caught hold of the baby lamb. Its skin was lined with ribs; as if it never sucked enough. She held it in her arms, petting its head, till the lamb stopped bleating, its body stopped shivering.

She sat in the dirt, in the moonlight, her back against a fencepost, cradling the lamb in her lap. Softly, she sang; a lullaby; singing it to sleep. The lamb nuzzled against her breast, getting settled. Nuzzled again, more insistently. With her left hand she unbottoned her blouse, to give the lamb the warmness of her skin. The lamb smelling of corral pressed inside the clean white cotton, snugly; and licked her soft nipple hard; and held with its moist lips, and suckled, trying to draw milk; till its head was wet with tears.

She sat for a long time, the lamb asleep in her lap. Till a mournful wind chilled her, and sent her inside. Shuddering, she wrapped in a blanket, and stared beyond thought at the dead fire's glow. When dawn finally broke, she slept.

The following afternoon the outfit returned, in a swirl of rickety pickups and children's shouts. The smiling sun and clear blue sky admitted no loss.

98

Her mother, kneeling beside the dark mound of earth, wept. Tinker stood beside her, silent.

Of the bottles in the dirt behind the door, they had no explanation. He had stopped drinking.

She didn't tell them the rest. About what the dog took. Bloody peach in dripping teeth. It made her sick, even now.

*****

Sirens whistled in her ears, blotting thought; the air above her pulsed blood-red, like a neon sign, on and off; puffs of blood-red lightning, seeking her in the night. Till the truck slowed, and stopped at the side of the road, the police car pulling up behind. Pulsing bloodlights over footsteps passing, and a gruff voice. "Let's see your license."

"The girl's sick. We're goin' to the hospital."

Footsteps crunched again, and the voice spoke close above, from a face blinking red and black.

"You sick?"

"Her baby's coming." Her mother's voice. "It's coming fast."

The face dissolved. The gruff voice barked louder. "Don't just sit there. Get movin'. The girl's havin' her baby!"

Gears screeched and the truck lurched forward, bumping her head, and gathered speed, leaving the bloodlights behind. Hurtling now, with approval. The wind whipping colder, her mother pulling a blanket tight; not knowing what was in her head. This closest person to her, knowing what was in her belly, but not the thoughts or memories that twisted and danced in her brain. Stroking her hair with love. Her closest stranger.

Twin ravens fluttered inside, as always. Sadness and happiness. Somber memories of dead things, entwined like vines with the sugar warmth of telling them. Telling them to him. To Michael. Sugar warmth that grew with the touch of his eyes.

They were in his living room one Sunday afternoon when she told of her father's death. Of the suckling lamb. When she finished, he said nothing. As if her life transported him to other worlds; into swimming pools of thought.

Winter twilight had seeped into the room as she talked, painting it gray: ceiling, floor, walls, books, furniture. Struggling for attention with the orange fire. Making its presence known in the gentle insistence of a low hum, a mild irritation: the phonograph needle scratching in the well. The record had ended minutes before. They hadn't noticed.

Michael lying on his stomach, face toward the fire, stood, and moved across the room in the deepening gray. A lamp ignited golden at his touch, pushing back the evening. He removed the record, soft piano music, the blue album with the funny name, De Pussy; and replaced it with another; and sat beside her on the rug, in the dark concave between glow of lamp and glow of fire. She sensed excitement in him, which blended a moment later with the music. It was Navajo music. The Blessing Way.

She turned from the suckling lamb that peered out of the flames. Her blood was warmed by the chant.

"Where did you find that?"

"I play it sometimes, at night. When you're not here."

Shyly, she smiled with her eyes, into his. Gently he moved his fingertips across her face. Across her lips. Lingering on her lips.

They kissed. For the first time. Lightly. Then harder. Her back was against the rug; the back of her head was on the rug; his face was above her, their lips were touching, pressing, her hand behind his head, her hand in his hair, lips caressing in a soft wet dance, the weight of his chest all firm and gentle on her breasts, kissing, kissing, kisses stirring new flashes of hunger, new spreading points of moisture, lower. In the dark between glow of lamp and glow of fire. In the chant of the Blessing Way.

The chant was over, the record was scratching again, when they pulled apart, faces flushed.

"It's getting late," he said. "We better go eat."

She awoke the next day in the dawn of a distant dream. She couldn't sleep. The narrow bed in the dormitory could hardly contain her. The walls, the floor, the desk, the chair, were singing; singing a song of Michael. Birds in the trees outside were whistling his name. The alarm clock on the bookshelf was ticking it: Mi / kel Mi / kel Mi / kel. Her blood tingled beneath her skin. Behind her eyes a morning dread was gone. In its place was a smiling calm. A blue serenity. A casual strength. An eagerness. She was eagle, ready to take wing on the wind of another day. To soar. To paint with a special vigor. For Michael, whom she would be seeing again that night. Once in a restaurant she had tasted his wine, and her head had floated high on clouds of sun. Now she was floating again, without any drink.

The feeling persisted, day after day. The first presence in her mind when she awoke each morning was Michael. The last presence in her mind each night as she smiled to sleep in the narrow bed was the unbelievable reality of Michael. The passion of each goodnight kiss heralded the next. Their talks, their jokes, the mingling of their hands, wove a blanket of trust that became her new fabric. She dwelled for the first time in a valley serene, free of snakes and lightning, free of thunder and wild dogs, free of scowling menace. The dangers of the world had fled; fled like beasts before a fire. She walked in the lightness of a dance, on solid ground; shoulders high; never stepping in holes that weren't there. There weren't any holes that weren't there.

There was no such thing as love. She knew that. Not the kind of love they showed in the movies, between boy and girl, between man and woman; love with flowers in the air and soft sweet music in the sky; not the kind of romantic love where people lived only for the moments they could be together. That kind of love was a lie, made up by businessmen, to sell soap, to sell toothpaste, to sell sprays for under the arms, to sell dyes to color the hair, to sell blades to shave the legs. To sell every product that made life unnatural. Her mother said so. Tinker said so. All of The People knew it. The reason you married someone, the reason you spent your life together, was so as not to be alone. You married someone who had many horses, or many sheep; who was a good worker, from a good family, who would keep a hogan over your head in case of a storm; who would earn bread for the children, because people needed sex, and children were the natural order. You would want to be together, because the world was a dangerous place, and it was scary to be alone. But love and violins like in the movies? That was a fantasy; a false promise, made up to sell cream for the face, and curlers for the hair.

So she was not in love.

But if not, what name could she give this new, outrageous feeling; this blue serenity?

She lived for their time together. For the sweet anticipation of their time together. For the lingering chocolate taste of their time together. She knew it was the same for him. In happiness they were united.

They went to the Turf Club, to hear country music. In the dark glow of candles in red vases the cowboy hats of farmers and ranchers floated like silhouette ships on a nighttime sea. During the slow tunes they danced, close.

They went to Pablo's for sopaipillas, and got none. (It was Monday, not Tuesday. Michael had forgotten what day it was.)

They went to Madrid, an old coal-mining town, abandoned now, decaying gray wooden houses peering from a hillside like rows of rotted teeth; climbed to an empty windowless church stripped bare that overlooked the dead but not buried town; kissed in shadows beneath the steeple, where long-gone coal miners once were christened, and married, and laid to rest. On the way back they saw up a dirt road a round plastic house like half a melon, gleaming white. "The house of the future," Michael said. "Scientists say it's the most efficient shape to build a house. It's called a geodesic dome." She slid closer to him on the seat. She tried not to smile.

"We call it a hogan," she said, and kissed him quickly on the neck.

They went with Buck to a basketball game in Albuquerque, Michael's old school Arizona State against the Lobos of New Mexico. She basked in their voices as Michael and Buck talked sports, and pulsed with the excitement of eighteen thousand people under one roof, more than the whole Navajo nation had been once, eighteen thousand people standing and screaming when a leather ball went through an iron hoop. A vast Anglo sand-painting, whose meaning remained obscure.

They saw each other every day for thirty days: for gobbled hamburgers when he was on duty at the hospital; at other times for quiet dinners and movies afterwards, holding hands; or just talks on the rug before the fire, ending with long, deep kisses; and goodnight pecks when he dropped her at the dorm. Afterwards, sometimes, lying in the narrow bed, she would rub herself moist with thoughts of him (dismissing tales of the old chiefs daughter who had rubbed herself with a cactus, and gotten children without any faces, without any arms).

She told him of the night she took the pills. Of the terror that burned her brain in the nights preceding. Merely talking of it, for the first time, eased the weight. She felt closer to him then to anyone, ever. She had no more secrets to hide under blankets of dark. Nothing more to fear.

She began to allow herself daydreams; gentle fantasies. Behind his house in the woods—which he had not yet bought; which he had not yet made any move to find—she added another, smaller cabin: her studio. She saw herself painting there all the day, while Michael was away at the hospital. In late afternoon, when the light was fading, she would stop painting, and build a fire in the main house, and cook dinner on the wood-burning stove. When she heard the jeep churning up the dirt road, she would run out to greet him (the Irish setter always getting there first). They would kiss, he would put his

103

arm around her, together they would walk to the cabin. Over dinner they would discuss the day's events. She would listen to his latest complaints about the hospital; about what he would do if he were in charge. When he was talked out she would lead him to the studio, and show him by floodlight the painting on which she was working. They would return to the cabin, and stretch out on a rug before the fire, the Irish setter sleeping nearby, and he would read to her, from whichever of his favorite books they were reading aloud: "The Brothers Karamazov," or "Moby Dick," or that funny one, "The Catcher in the Rye." Getting sleepy, they would undress, and climb into bed, naked under a big downy quilt. The nearness of each other's flesh would give them new energy to make beautiful love; till they drifted off to sleep, her head nestling in his shoulder.

Sometimes, if she were fantasizing at night, as she lay waiting for sleep in her narrow bed, she would dwell much longer on the love-making part. Would see herself spread, squatting above him, the ends of her hair dancing on his chest.

When she was not daydreaming she was painting; painting better than ever, because she was painting for him. Her favorite, done in one long week of work, skipping classes, skipping meals, showed the towering rock people of the valley, her friends from childhood, not burning this time, not spaced across the landscape as in reality, but lined up in neat rows in the foregound, like cars at a drive-in movie. In the middle distance was a large movie screen, and on it was a self-portrait, her hands holding her dark hair piled high on her head, like a movie star. It was the first self-portrait she had done in which she was not a child herding sheep. Surrounding the rock people was barren desert. Surrounding the movie screen was starry night. In the lower right-hand corner, spelled in an oval of lights on a movie marquee, was the name of the picture that was playing: "Home Town Girl."

The image, bursting full-blown from her unconscious, touched a special chord. She had left the reservation; she had crossed the bridge of lies that was uncrossable; she had given up the protection of the valley; she had moved into the white man's world her father hated so; and had found there an unknown strength, a purer happiness. Michael. A century of lies, cheating, wars, massacres, broken promises, never to be forgotten, melted nonetheless into recesses; into the musty pages of history texts. The end product, for her, for now, was just the two of them. The twining of their fingers. The brushing of their lips. She and Michael.

The merging of their bodies would come soon. She could sense it building. She knew that she must wait, patiently. She knew that clocks were ticking, everywhere. In his pulse. In his chest. In his belly. And in hers.

*****

Early spring pushed winter out the door. On a mild Sunday afternoon they went for dinner to friends of Michael's, Tom and Phoebe Gaddis. Michael had mentioned Tom, he taught at the College of Santa Fe. She had never met them. The afternoon there passed as through a Chinese screen: muted, delicate, at times a little fuzzy (they had served a wine punch). She was aware of three young children moving about, two girls and a boy, behaving nicely. She was aware of good food, rice with chicken and shrimp in it, and sweet dessert. She was aware of pleasant conversation across the table, and in the adobe living room, she mostly listening, speaking when asked a question, speaking more as the visit lasted. But later, her heart beating wildly, she could remember no word of what had been said. The talk disappeared in the one overwhelming fact of the afternoon; the overwhelming screen of her perception; the blow that had struck her weak when Phoebe Gaddis first had come to the door. Phoebe was Indian! They had been married seven years. Phoebe was a potter, not a painter, her husband was a teacher, not a doctor. Small change. Phoebe was the living, laughing flesh of her own fantasies, the proof that it could be done. And Michael had taken her there.

He dropped her early at the dorm. It was his night to telephone his daughter, long distance. In her room her throbbing heartbeat pounded on the walls. The Blessing Way. She grinned herself silly in the mirror on the wall. Wanted to hug herself. And did. Unrolled her canvases, tossed them one by one from the bed to the floor, studying each. Narrowed the choice to two: the new one, her self-portrait on the movie screen amid the rock people; and an older one he liked, an eagle soaring high above the desert. She chose the eagle. Eagle was how he said he felt when he used to walk in the desert outside Tuba. She would give him himself.

She rolled the other canvases and stood them in the darkness of the closet. Separately she rolled the eagle, and taped it with masking tape. She placed it on the bed, and sat at her desk. Carefully, in a lined spiral notebook, skipping a line between each line she wrote, she began to compose a note with a thick drawing pen.

Dear Michael,

It might be the wine punch that is making me write this. But I don't think so. It is only my happiness.

I want you to have this painting. May your spirit always fly like an eagle. I hope you like it.

She put down the pen, and read the note. With a rush, the excitement of a new idea drew lines in her head. She continued writing.

I wish I had money to buy you a nice present. Since I don't, there is something else I want to give. A long time ago, you asked me my Navajo name. I said I couldn't tell you, that it was a secret, to be used only in sacred chants. But tonight I feel as close to you as to any Navajo. So I want you to know my name.

She started to write the name, but lifted the pen. She couldn't decide if it needed to be explained. She chewed on the end of the pen, and stood and

106

paced the room, and looked out the window at the empty campus. Everyone must be in their rooms, studying. She sat again, and took up the pen, and wrote.

When I was little, I loved to eat chocolate, and all kinds of candy. Anything made of sugar. The old people a long time ago had no word for sugar. When they first got it from the white men, they had to make up a word. So they called it sweet salt.

When they saw me eating candy all the time, that is what they named me. Sweet Salt.

She chewed on the pen again, a vein throbbing in her temple. Her hand trembled as she wrote one more paragraph, the letters more squiggly than before.

I wish I had a better gift to give you, but that is all I have. That and what I feel.

She signed the note "Nina." She read it several times, in the golden circle of the gooseneck lamp, feeling her blouse clinging. She drew a line through "Nina." Underneath it, she signed: "Sweet Salt."

She folded the note, and put it in an envelope. She took it out and read it again. She put it in the middle drawer of the desk. And took it out again. Life-force rushing inside her egged her on. There would be no sleeping till the note was delivered. She read it one more time. Put it in the envelope. Licked the envelope, grimacing at the taste. Taped it to the outside of the canvas. Flushed and shivering, she pulled on her coat, and hurried down the stairs, carrying the rolled canvas. She crossed the parking lot to the hospital. A knot of people was standing inside the entrance in the dim green light, talking with their hands. A car had smashed into a power pole on the Albuquerque highway. The driver had broken the windshield with his face. They had taken him to St. Vincent's, the hospital across town. They were trying to save his eyes.

She felt faint, and clutched at the wall. The moment passed. She hurried down the hall.

The door to his office was open. In the dim light she found his desk, covered with papers and folders, and a crumpled pack of cigarettes that made her smile. Careful not to disturb his papers, she placed the rolled canvas across his desk, the envelope toward the front. She wished she hadn't sealed it. Wished she could read it one more time. To make sure how she felt. And knew she was being absurd. She knew the note by heart. Had written it by heart.

She left it, and walked down the hall, perspiring, and out into the night. The knot of people discussing the injured man had vanished.

*****

The next morning, with cold still to come, spring blossomed prematurely into the warmth of summer. From her window she saw people crossing the campus carrying their coats instead of wearing them; caterpillars shedding cocoons against the slight green fuzz of newborn grass. She skipped breakfast, stayed in the dorm till the last moment, sitting restlessly, first on the bed, then on the chair, then on the bed again, hoping Michael would call when he found the painting. Till she realized that of course he wouldn't. He would assume she was in class. She hurried, and slid into her seat just as the bell rang.

The classrooms were different that day: the seats harder than ever, the wood and metal replaced by rock. The clocks had been changed: the hands of the clocks now dragged great weights with desperate slowness uphill toward the 12; then dropped them, only to start over again, deliberate, maddening. The teachers spoke in a verbal haze, sentences melting into the liquid ringing of faraway telephones. By mid-afternoon she couldn't stand it any longer. She cut her last class, and ran, breathless, back to the dormitory.

She stopped at the switchboard, to tell the girl on duty she would be in her room, in case there were any calls. "I think there's a message," the girl said. "A few minutes ago." The girl riffled a pink message pad, tore out a page and handed it to her. It had her name on top, and underneath it said: "Michael called. Wants you to meet him in Plaza at 5 o'clock."

She looked at the back of the paper. There was nothing on it. "That's all?" she said. "No other message?"

"That's it," the girl said.

A caged tiger waiting for feeding time. She paced in the narrow room. Nothing about the painting, or the note. Of course not. He would tell her in person.

She thought of running to his office across the parking lot. But dared not. He must be busy. He had his reasons.

Why the Plaza? To catch the waning sun after a day indoors. To tell her something special, in a special place. In the heart of the city. He was romantic that way. At 5 o'clock the Plaza would be crowded with people leaving work, but a few minutes after it would be deserted. They could twine their fingers on a white iron bench, and be alone in historic stillness; could whisper glances and secret smiles in the privacy of space.

The Plaza, then.

It was a little more than a mile. She put on a fresh blouse, and carried a sweater. She walked the pavement of Cerrillos Road, against the flow of increasing traffic. Past the busy businesses, bric-a-brac of the world the white man chose to build. She reached the Plaza at twenty minutes to 5, and sat on a bench gleaming white. She stretched her arms along the back of the bench, and leaned back her head, and shut her lids; letting the lover sun kiss her on the eyes.

The darkness of her lids flared orange. The sun warmed her face, chest, arms. People-noises spun around her in a backdrop melody. Till a real melody cut through it, the high melodic line of a clarinet. She opened her

109

eyes and through a sunblind haze saw a man in blue jeans and navy blue shirt—both seeming black through orange eyes—leaning against a tree across the Plaza, blowing a thin black horn. The music rose through the still-bare branches of trees, up toward the whitish blue sky, then seemed to curl like smoke over the roof of the Palace of the Governors, and disappear in dark clouds hovering over the silent snow-crested Sangre de Cristos beyond.

She closed her eyes again, giving herself to the music and the orange-luring sun. Till a voice spoke close to her ear.

"Sleeping Beauty?"

She started, frightened, opening her eyes to the dark shape looming near.

"Michael!"

He sat beside her on the white iron bench.

"What's the matter?"

"Nothing." Searching for lost breath. "You startled me. My head was somewhere else."

"Where?"

"I don't know. Somewhere up in the clouds, with the music."

"Been waiting long?"

"Not very. Is it 5 o'clock yet?"

"Almost."

She twined her fingers through his. "You left the hospital early?" He had been so eager to see her; to tell her.

He looked down, the way he did when he was shy, or pained, then looked up again. Pausing. His eyes roamed the Plaza. "I didn't go to the hospital today. I called in sick."

Her heart sank to her belly. He hadn't seen it. It was still there, rolled up on his desk; meaningless, till he saw it, as toilet paper. The eagle. Her note. Sweet Salt.

"What is it? Are you really sick?"

110

Again his eyes avoided her, and looked at the ground. "No. Not physically sick."

She shuddered with chill, as if the sun had gone behind a cloud. It hadn't. Her heart in her belly twisted claws. A dull ache started in her stomach. Her brain, easy and flowing sweet wine these past days / weeks / months, began to clench. His voice spoke premonitions. Michael Kitcarson.

"Michael, what's the matter?" The panic was not in his face. It was in her throat.

He squeezed her hand. Both their palms were sweaty.

"Nina ... I can't see you anymore. We can't see each other anymore."

"Why not?" Her heart was sinking lower, leaving her belly. "What did I do? Did I do something wrong?"

He looked into her face. Ran his finger along her eyebrow. Sighed a dying sigh. "Nina; Nina; Nina." Shaking his head. "It's not you. It's me."

"Michael, what is it? Tell me!"

He let go of her hand. Looked down, and then up again; searching for words in the air. "I've gotten too involved with you."

She couldn't stop her smile. Sweet warmth slowed the draining of her blood. "I know that." Words flowed trippingly in her brain. They were not spoken quite so easily. They came out shyer than she expected. Softer. "I've gotten involved with you, too."

"You don't understand."

He searched for his words on the ground. She was aware of a change in the pattern of movement around them. Footsteps going home from work had been replaced by footsteps swirling past them, toward the Palace of the Governors beyond.

"What is there to understand?"

"I lie awake all night, thinking about you." Again she couldn't stop her smile. "I can't continue like this."

"Continue like what?"

111

"I want to make love to you."

She bit back budding tears of joy. She rested her arm on his shoulder. He seemed relieved to have said what he said. Her own words were softer, shyer, than she expected.

"Michael, I'm here. Waiting. Whenever you want."

He turned his face to her. "Nina, don't. We can't, you know we can't."

For a moment the world seemed absurd; as if she were trapped in a madman's dreams. People passing by, the two of them talking like this in the center of the city. A flicker of anger stirred inside her.

"Why can't we, if we want?"

He didn't answer. A shaft of sunlight broke through her confusion. She squeezed his arm. "Don't worry, it won't be...my first time. "You're forgetting Robert."

"Robert was different." He leaned forward, elbows on his thighs, looking at the ground between his shoes. "Robert was the same age as you. Robert was a student, like you. You could do whatever you wanted. Nobody cared."

Anger cut her like a knife. "You mean Robert was an Indian, like me."

His head jerked up as if pulled by a string. He looked her hard in the face. His words were measured, pained. "You know that isn't true."

She threw her arms around his shoulders, pressed her wet face into his neck. "I'm sorry, Michael, I'm sorry." The words coming muffled in his collar and his neck. "I know it's not true, you've got me all confused. I don't know what I'm saying." She raised her head, sniffling to clear her face. "Michael... I love you." Sobs jabbing her words. "I think you love me, too."

His arms enfolded, comforting. Held her till the crying stopped.

"I'm sorry," she said. She wiped her eyes with her hands.

A large crowd had formed across the Plaza; was lining the street in front of the Palace of the Governors, waiting for something. Latecomers were hurrying to join the crowd. Some were priests in black, carrying white silk robes. The people were looking at the entrance. She and Michael, on the

112

white iron bench across the Plaza, were being ignored. She was grateful at least for that.

He started to speak again, holding her hand. His words came slowly. "I can't stand hurting you. It's the most painful thing I've ever had to do."

"Then . . ."

"Let me finish. I guess my thoughts were in my head so much, I assumed you knew them. I guess I haven't explained very well."

She waited.

"I'm 32 years old. You're 17. That's almost twice your age."

"But.. "

"Listen to me. Okay? You're 17. That doesn't stop me from . . . caring for you. But it stops me from making love to you."

"Michael, that's crazy. What about Robert? I was only 16 then."

"You were students, nobody cared. Think how it looks from the outside. I'm a doctor, an Anglo. At the Indian hospital. You're a student. A Navajo. How did we meet? I was treating you. You were my patient. I was treating you after you took pills. After . . . you know. You start coming to my office, to talk about your problems—and I start making love to you. You know how that would look, if anyone found out?"

"What does it matter how it looks? It only matters how we feel."

Wild images reared in her brain, mustangs thundering through a canyon, coyotes slinking at the edge of a pinon-dotted slope, eagles gliding in the blue, sheep munching sage, rabbits scurrying, dogs barking, cattle lowing, roosters crowing, copper boys on stallions with flaring nostrils shooting arrows into the invisible distance, all of them, every last creature, gray—gray and trapped behind bars. Gray and trapped in a shadow death.

"Maybe it shouldn't matter, but it does. You know what they would do? They would kick me out of the hospital. They would kick me out of the Public Health Service. They could even take away my license. They could stop me from being a doctor."

113

"Nobody has to know."

"People would know. They always find out. We'd want to be together all the time. At night. . ."

"Michael! What if we got married! There's no law against that!"

She could hardly believe what she had said.

"There's no law. Except what you're forgetting. I'm still married. A divorce takes time . . . even if we wanted to. You're 17, Nina. You've got your whole life ahead of you. Your painting. You don't want to get married yet."

From the crowd behind them, music started. Mariachi music that she hated. They both turned to look. They couldn't see the musicians. They were somewhere in the crowd.

She sat in the dripping silence of voiceless clocks.

"What is it you want me to do? Can't we just go on like we've been, and see what happens?"

"That's what I've been doing for weeks. Going on like we've been. I can't any more. You know why I asked you to meet me here?"

She shook her head.

"Because I didn't dare be alone with you. Because I know what would have happened."

She grabbed his arm; a straw in the water. "Let's go, now," she whispered.

"Nina, I can't. It's my whole life at stake. I can't."

There was weariness in his words. And defeat. A shudder of lightning, illuminating wreckage.

"Then I won't see you again? Ever?"

The words sounded dumb. As from a movie. Without meaning. Like saying: I won't see the sun again, ever. Or the sky.

"That's how it has to be."

She was drained. Could think of no more words. Welcomed a loud cheer when it rose from the crowd behind them across the Plaza. Together they feigned interest; put on masks they had long since discarded. Walked tight-muscled, weak-kneed, in the failing light of dark clouds, to the edge of the crowd; peering through masks with half an eye; trying to escape an ingrown wail; trembling. Michael asked a man what was happening. The man was Spanish. She saw that most of the crowd was Spanish. "The new archbishop is being installed," the man said.

The crowd near the entrance parted. The mariachis were wearing ugly blue uniforms, and sombreros with tassels hanging. A man in a black tophat waved the crowds back, till the people were lining the curbs. A man walked out of the entrance, wearing white silk robes, carrying a white curved stick like a shepherd's staff. He was about 40 years old, Spanish, with dark hair and kind eyes. Behind him walked a double line of priests. The people lining the curbs applauded and cheered. "Peace and love," a man called out. The archbishop smiled, and waved his hand.

The procession wended around the Plaza, toward the Cathedral a block away. Children ran into the street to the archbishop. He shook their hands, or patted their heads, smiling. The adults seemed to want to rush forward also, to have their heads patted. They didn't dare. They stood on the curb, waving, applauding.

Raindrops began to fall from the dark clouds overhead. She and Michael crossed the street, and stood under the portal in front of a dress shop. The people lining the curbs joined the procession behind the line of priests. Slowly the procession moved toward the cathedral. The marchers were getting wet. Nobody ran, or seemed to mind the rain.

The drops grew heavier, bouncing off the bricks like waterflowers. The last marchers had passed through the Plaza, going to Mass in the cathedral. The square was empty now, except for wet trees, wet benches, wet bricks; and the two of them, dry under the portal. Dry inside their masks. She felt alone; more alone than she had felt in months. All those people. All those strangers. Come together for a man they didn't know. Come and gone; the empty Plaza left in the futile gladness of a parade that has passed.

The rain tapered and stopped as suddenly as it had begun. The air was heavy with the smell of ripe fruit, rotting.

"I'll drive you back to the dorm," Michael said.

They rode in silence. At the parking lot they both got out. He put his hands on her shoulders, to kiss her goodbye. She pulled his hands away.

"A long time ago," she said, "you told me about the Navajos and the Jews. About the things we have in common."

He waited, looking puzzled.

"You know what the main difference is? I bet you don't even know."

He seemed unable to speak. He could only look at her, as if waiting to be slapped.

"You have books," she said. "We have songs."

He didn't respond. She turned, and walked across the parking lot; walking faster as she neared the building; running up the steps, hot tears running down her cheeks.

When she peered from the window, he was gone.

*****

In time the tears stopped. She went to sleep, tossing beneath the blanket. Slept all night in her clothes, as she did at home. Went to class in the morning without changing. Shuffled through the day in herds of fog. After class she found a sealed envelope in her box. From Michael. He had found her canvas, and her note. He was deeply moved. Perhaps, under the circumstances, he should return the painting. But he would like to keep it. To treasure it, always. To have something of hers with him, always. Just as she would always have something of his. A piece of his heart. P.S.—Please, it would be easier, if she didn't answer this note.

116

She crumpled the note and threw it into a basket. She started up the stairs to her room. She went down, and fished the note out of the basket, and shoved it into the pocket of her jeans.

It was 3 o'clock. Below her window the sun was shining brightly over the campus. She went to sleep.

*****

A change in the rhythm of the truck brought her back. As if some destiny was approaching. She opened her eyes. Her mother was sitting up, staring into the flat dark distance. The truck seemed to have slowed.

"Mama, are we almost there?"

Her mother turned, looking down at her, and squeezed her arm. "A few more minutes. The turnoff is up ahead." She gazed again to the beyond. To her own private thoughts.

Nina spread her fingers on the blanket, till she found Tinker's handkerchief. She clenched it in a coldsweat palm; pulled up her skirt, letting draft swirl in; pressed the handkerchief to sticky wool; pulled it out again from beneath her skirt. It was covered with black blood. Red black in the dark. She pushed the handkerchief under the blanket; so her mother wouldn't see.

"If the baby lives, I want it to be a boy. Which do you want, mama?"

Her mother looked down, and stroked her forehead. "It doesn't matter. I wouldn't mind a little girl like you."

If the baby lives. Envisioning a twisted, strangled fetus, bathed in black blood; with the head of a barking dog. Shuddering; forcing her mind away.

"When the baby is born," her mother said, "will you tell us the father?"

"I told you twenty times. There is no father. The sky, the valley, the rock people. These will be the father. I will love my baby myself. Enough for a hundred fathers."

Her mother sighed; frustration in her breath.

117

"Mama, please! It will be okay."

She didn't want to talk any more. She closed her eyes; shut out her mother, the stars, the truck. Went back to Santa Fe. To the night of her long walk. To the night her baby began.

She remembered she was in the dorm. Alone in her room, on a Saturday night. For three weeks she had waited. Waited for Michael to call. Certain he would get lonely. That he would call, just to talk. To see how she was. That they would start in over again. For three weeks she waited. Cutting classes, to be in her room in case he called. Gazing out the window at the top of his jeep, parked in the hospital parking lot. Sometimes catching a glimpse of him leaving the hospital, getting into the jeep, driving off; the window ledge for an instant spinning dizzily at such moments. Fighting with all her strength the desire to cross the hundred yards of asphalt; to go to his office; or to be waiting outside when he came out. Just once. To say hello. Knowing-it wasn't just once to say hello. Fearing that he would be angry. That if he were breaking down, that if he were getting ready to call her, she would ruin it all. Once she couldn't stop herself. She sat on the hospital steps at a quarter to five; waiting to see him when he came out; a lame excuse in her mind; she was waiting for a friend from school. The waiting was torment, her mind a twist of nerves. She waited alone on the steps till 7 o'clock. He didn't come out. She stood, and looked for his jeep in the parking lot. It wasn't there. She hadn't thought to look if it was there when she came. He had left early, or he hadn't worked that day. She trembled all over. She never went again to sit on the steps.

She listed through classes with half an ear, half an eye. She couldn't paint, and when she tried, she painted badly, dark colors one atop the other, till they were mud. She had little appetite for food. When his jeep was in the parking lot she sat by the window, watching it; hypnotized. When it wasn't there, she slept.

118

The third Saturday she stayed in the room all day, not wanting food. When darkness fell she did not turn on a light, but sat in the dark by the window, watching a full moon rising. There was a dance at the gym that night. Music of pounding drums and electric guitars pulsed across the campus. Couples passed beneath her window, laughing. Her skin and muscles crawled from lack of exercise. She had to get out of the room, could not stand it any longer. Decided to wait ten more minutes—to 9 o'clock—in case he called.

She would change her clothes, go out; somewhere. She stripped in the dark. Heard more laughing couples passing by. She peered out the window, hiding her body against the wall. She had a wild impulse, wanted to push her chair to the window, stand up on the chair, wanted to spread her legs, spread her arms, lean her naked body against the cool glass, facing outward; wanted to give herself to the green glow of the moon, hope that the laughing couples below would look up on their way to the dance, would see her, mooncolor by moonlight, her spread legs, perfect triangle of midnight warm, full heavy breasts, chocolate nipples distended now at the thought, leaving the boys aching, forgetting mortal girls they had brought along. Yellow-Evening-Light-Girl. Changing Woman. Sweet Salt.

Her heart was palpitating. She moved away from the window, and sat on the bed. She was sickened by how real the impulse had been. How mad the desire.

She pulled down the black window shade, and switched on the lamp on the desk. The clock said 9:15. She found clean panties in her drawer, fresh jeans and a clean yellow blouse in her closet. She dressed in a corner of the room; so she would cast no shadow on the shade.

She had to get out; had to stretch her muscles or go mad; but she was not going near his house. She was not going near his house because it was a Saturday night, and he probably would be out. The house would be dark, and the jeep would be missing. In which case there was no reason not to go near his house—to pass by, on the other side of the street—and see that the house was dark, and the jeep was missing; and be able to put him out of her mind, for the rest of the night. If she did not start wondering where he was.

The couples had disappeared, into the human noises of the gym, or into the night. Music strained through basketball hoops lapped at the base of campus trees like tired tide. Crossing the unborn lawns, she pulled her sweater on. April days were warm, but night still whispered goosebumps on the skin.

At the gate she turned left, toward town. For a moment she hesitated, telling herself to be strong, to go the other way. But that way lay nothing but three miles of roadside clutter, closed at night except for McDonald's or Dairy Queen, and after that nothing but rolling, sloping, pinon-studded desert, clear to Albuquerque. She could walk for days that way, out into the desert, meeting no one, seeing no living creature, till one day a low-flying helicopter spotted her bleached bones.... She cut the internal recital. The drama was making her worse. It was not that kind of desert. She moved off to the left, toward town; because that's where she wanted to go. Headlights on Cerrillos Road droned toward her, slowly, pinpoints; then faster, brighter; bathed her face and body with twin searchlights, or the sharp interrogation lights of police; blinded her for an instant to the sockets; then rushed by with a puff of air and the hum of motor noise, leaving her eyes to recover on the narrow walk; till the next pair of empty lights came searching out her eyes.

She turned left again at the first chance, at St. Francis Drive. Passed an orchard of trees with upraised branches that reminded her now of prisoners surrendering. Crossed the wide street quickly through a darkness in the traffic. Walked in the same direction as the cars, following red tail lights that winked and dipped and rose again, leading her to the neighborhood where Michael lived, in the three-bedroom house he had made no move to sell.

Still another left and she was on streets that were smaller, darker, with no cars except those that were parked at the curb. Suburban-style houses with jeeps or station wagons in the driveways stood side by side on small plots with old adobes, some crumbling, others newly restored. Newcomers assumed that Anglos lived in the modern brick houses, and Spanish in the old adobes. Often it was the reverse. The Spanish who grew up here were seeking progress. The Anglos who moved here were seeking roots. The houses were set back by bits of lawn that in the summer sprouted grass and flowers neatly tended by mothers of school-age children. Narrow strips of earthgrass ran beside the houses to the rear, where they opened into slightly larger back lawns decorated with children's swings and jungle gyms, the back yards surrounded by goat fences, to keep dogs in, or out.

Without conscious choice her feet were taking her; a horse that knows the way; under webs of trees that fractured the cut-glass moon; into clearings of skydark that made it whole again; to the base of a hill that fell away, leaving the broad flat belly of the city exposed to view, lined with lights, soft random lights of porches and living rooms, sharp white lights of streets, spreading in three directions, making the city seem larger at night than it was by day, till the lights were swallowed in the great black abutment of the mountains, still as a dead lover under the full moon rising.

Her heart pounded racily in her chest. The street climbing behind her was lined on both sides with houses. Halfway up on the right-hand side was Michael's.

She dared not go further. What if he were home? What would she say? She tried to imagine his face when he found her at the door. Pain and puzzlement; followed by a false show of welcome. Or would he hug her close, whisper her name, his lips touching her hair in a summer breeze?

He would not be home.

She crossed the street to the far side. Wished the moon were not so bright, so no one would see her; though no one was in the street. Slowly dragged reluctant leaden thighs up the hill; stepping carefully; heart beating quicker still; and peered across. Houses with warm rectangles of ochre lights seemed to alternate with houses dark. She couldn't tell which was his.

A skulking thief, she re-crossed in mid-block, looking both ways into the stillness. She stepped onto the curb—and found herself facing the squat back of his jeep, parked in the driveway. She was less than twenty feet from the door to his house. Behind closed blinds in the wide window a lamp glowed, inviting; enticing; unnerving.

She tried to call up her courage. Courage had drained through the soles of her feet to a river underground. She wanted to leave, to run through the night before her face was seen. She found herself moving forward, carried by legs obeying some predetermined will. She tried to think. Thought was drowned in the blood-red pounding of her chest.

She stood in a pool of amber light from a square bulb above the door. She found her hand on the bell, obeying the same outside will. She heard chimes ringing far away; inside the house. Electric shock of chimes stiffened her body. Her muscles pulled together, her brain cleared. Courage reversed its flow, moving upward now, coursing through her veins. It would only be Michael. Michael whom she loved. She felt strong, strong as the rock people. A bold painter, a painter of reds and blacks. She pressed the bell again, harder. She was bred of a race of survivors. There was hope.

She wished she had dressed better; though it had never mattered before.

She listened for his footsteps. And was startled instead by the clicking of the lock. The dark door swung back half way. Around it peered an unknown face. The face of a woman, white, with pale blue eyes, and tangled blonde hair. The hair was wet, and stringy. The woman's hand, flashing white out of an orange robe, was holding a towel to it. Shoulders and breasts covered by the robe peered around the door.

"Can I help you?"

The voice was one-third annoyance, two-thirds polite. The orange robe was Michael's. She had seen it in his room.

She stared through the screen door. Her voice had left her. The bulb above the door became an X-ray machine, exposing her bones; exposing her misery.

The door opened further. The woman stood full behind the screen. The robe ended at her knees. Her feet were bare. From behind her came the sound of a shower running.

"Are you looking for someone?"

The woman was tall, calm, pretty. Like the models in magazines.

The sound of the shower stopped. Startled, she looked above the door.

"I'm sorry. I was looking for a friend. I must have the wrong house."

The woman nodded, and smiled, and put a hand on the doorknob, waiting for her to leave. She didn't move. The woman shrugged, and stepped back.

"Is there anything else?"

She shook her head. The woman shrugged again, and closed the door, slowly. The latch clicked. She stood, motionless, staring at the door under the X-ray light; as if it was a car door closing on her finger, and she couldn't move her hand. After several seconds, in a puff of silence, the light snuffed out.

Her knees felt shaky as she moved down the walk. Two dimes of moonlight blocked her path. Cat eyes. They stared at one another in the darkness.

The cat wouldn't move. She stamped her foot. The cat flinched, but held its ground; as if winning a point. Then it slunk away, and rippled its body like a thick snake under a white Beetle parked beside the curb.

The house floated behind her with its ochre rectangles and naked bodies under orange robes. Receded into some dark hogan of her brain; a color snapshot filed in a computer, evermore to be vomited up at the flick of a thought. Snapshot of life on a distant planet. Before her the dread city spread, lifeless lights twinkling and swimming now through the salt water shimmering in her eyes.

She couldn't cry. The tears in her head leaked out through her sockets, but wouldn't fall. They grew inward instead. And turned to something else.

Unerring, unseeing, legs leading the way, she walked the maze of residential streets. Came again to the broad modern paving of St. Francis Drive. Started across, sightless, to the hum of motor noise. Was between two lanes when headlights shrieked. She looked into the bowels of approaching whiteness; and couldn't move. In either lane she could die.

The earth cracked open. A great brown mouth beckoned. The gritty undergound of nothing. An egg that was only shell. Unfinished paintings danced around her, the bloody teeth of a yawn. They didn't matter any more. Nothing mattered any more. As in a dance she turned her side to death, accepting. And was not afraid. A swift, clean ending.

The headbeams caught her. The car swerved to the right. Wind whipped her blouse as the car blew by, inches away; freezing them together, bull and matador. The car hit the curb, bounced back to the middle, sped down the highway, down and out of sight. No driver's curses drifted back on the wind. Already it was too far for that. The driver who almost killed her would forever be unknown.

She finished crossing the drive, her knees growing soft. A survivor. Beyond the pavement on the far side was a black iron fence; and beyond that a cemetery, tombstones in every direction, glowing eerie in the moon. She pressed her face against the fence, as at the window of a restaurant filled with well-dressed diners eating mutton. Thought how sweet it would be to curl on a sheepskin of earth; to pull a blanket of fresh grass snugly to her neck; to pull it further, over her head; to sleep, forever. She was not afraid of death. She knew that, now. Of the dead, yes. The dead had ghosts, who could harm those left alive. But not of death. Death was the natural order.

A night-sky of sparks exploded in her brain. Somehow, in some way, Michael was like her father. She hammered the sparks to dark again. Hammered them away with the rhythm of the nerves that made her shake.

124

Her legs in their new authority carried her down a wide street lined on both sides with businesses. Automobile lots, each with dozens of cars huddling like overgrown frightened rabbits. Cars in each lot looking alike, family huddling with family, tribe with tribe. Beyond the car lots, cafes, closed for the night. A liquor store, whiskey monuments rising in tiers of brown and beige. A squat white building that claimed to be a newspaper office. Below a second-floor window, a wooden sign proclaiming: "Hand-Crafted Furniture." A Japanese word over a row of shiny motorcycles lined up like a chrome centipede making a turn.

Across another street a low sprawling building of fake adobe, covering an entire block. Calling itself the Santa Fe Hilton. The sign had a large red H on it. It reminded her of a sign that had a large red S on it, a sign that hung on the wall above the blackboard in the early years of school at Kayenta. The sign was a poem they had had to memorize in the second grade, and recite aloud one morning each week, like the pledge of allegiance. She still remembered the words:

> Success will not come
> To those who shirk;
> To get up in the world
> Get down to work.

They had learned the words but they didn't know what they meant. They didn't know who this Success was that was supposed to come. And where else could you get up if not in the world. And yet from somewhere, great yellow engines had begun to drive inside her, to drive her away from those who were satisfied with a full belly and a growing herd, as The People long had been, driving her to draw, driving her to paint, driving her toward some unknown destination that was written on the yellow engine, a destination she couldn't read, a large blue S, S for Sheep or S for Santa Fe. Driving her to Michael. A town where nobody lived.

*****

She followed the pavement as it snaked around the curved front of the building, and let it spit her through fangs of black glass into the bulbless white light of a carpeted lobby. A painted sign marked Conquistador Lounge, twin sister to one outside, pointed down a narrow corridor. She moved through the passageway, beneath round iron chandeliers fitted with glowing yellow bulbs in the pointy pregnant shape of candle flames. Tin music fell from hidden speakers— impotent remains of castrated popular songs. Along the left wall a bank of boothless pay telephones was set in sprays of Mexican tile; offering no privacy, but paying homage to local culture.

Formless chatter blew and spun like tumbleweed through the open door of the lounge. With slight hesitation, as if bracing herself against an ungaugable breeze, she stepped into the alien dark. People-shapes like cardboard cutouts surrounded round tables. Yellow smoke hung above them in the artificial flames. On a raised platform sleeping brass instruments beamed sharp slivers of moon. The band was taking a break.

She moved unnoticed in the coiled spaces between the tables to a polished bar at the far end of the large room, where the flameless yellow flames were trapped in silver mirrors. Out of place, but wanting— needing—a drink, she slipped onto a pink leatherette stool flanked by empty ones. Across the flat pink circle to her right a man in a dark blue suit and a woman in a black dress were seated, talking with their foreheads almost touching, drinks forgotten on the bar in front of them. Across the pimpled pink moon to her left a fat man sat, in a gray suit and a white shirt with no tie, three chins rolling down his red neck toward his chest, where gluttony was echoed in rolls of fat that folded over his belt. His face was pink as the empty stool, and his puffy fist was curled around a glass that seemed to disappear inside it. The man was gazing at the shirtfront of a skinny bartender, who had a thin face and graying hair and was wearing a short yellow jacket and a black bow

126

tie, and looked like an underfed bumblebee. The bartender held a rag with both hands, and was polishing beer glasses.

"So they went out to the arroyo, about five miles south of town," the bartender was saying, "and sure enough, there was a girl lying there. About seventeen years old, pretty as a picture. Stark naked, and blonde from head to toe. Stark dead, too."

"Wouldna minded finden that one myself," the fat man said, with a chuckle that seemed to be born and die in his thick throat, without ever escaping to life in the world outside.

"They had no idea who she was," the bartender said. "No clothing, no identification. Not even a ring. Nothing at all to go by. So they brought her in, and the autopsy showed. . .

"Brought her in?" the fat man said. "Shit. I saw a movie once, where this dick comes to a motel, and finds this chick lyin' face down on the bed. Natural redhead, built like a brick shithouse. He touches her, but she doesn't move. She's out cold. So he figures he'll grab in a quickie. He drops his drawers, and does his stuff, right in from the back. Then he turns her over, to let her in on the surprise. And what do ya know? She's got a neat round bullet hole right in the middle of her forehead. Dick finds out he just laid a corpse. Not that the chick looked bad, even dead."

"Yeah, well that's in the movies," the bartender said. She was squirming uncomfortable on the stool, her jeans starting to stick to the leatherette, and the bartender gave her the flicker of a glance, as if to say I'll be with you in a minute. But he kept polishing the beer glasses and talking to the man.

"The point is, they don't know who this girl is. She's got no name. How can they look for a killer when they don't know who the victim is? So they take a Polaroid picture of the body—color, no less—and they start showing it around town, asking if anybody ever seen her. And where do they start looking? In the bars. Figured maybe somebody picked her up hitchin' —all these kids running away from home and all. They come in here on a Saturday night. The place is jammed, everybody having a good time, the cash register ringing, and the sheriff says, 'Quiet down, everybody. We got this picture of a dead girl, we got to show it around.' Can you beat that? The place buzzed for a minute, then quiets down like a morgue. One by one everybody looks at the picture, and shakes their heads. Nobody knows her. The sheriff says thanks for their trouble, and leaves—just like that—and I'm left with the deadest bunch of Saturday night crowd I ever seen. Something like that puts a damper on a party. It was a good hour before that bunch got goin' again. Don't know how much in tips I lost. Can I help you, miss?"

He had moved down the bar as she listened. The question caught her by surprise.

"I'd like a Coors," she said, her voice dry with nerves.

"You got eye dee?"

She stared at the white on his bumblebee chest, as if she hadn't heard. Hoping he wouldn't pursue it.

"I said you got eye dee? Driver's license?"

She looked at him blankly, and then with difficulty pulled her wallet out of her pocket. She fumbled through her papers, looking for the license that wasn't there. Her hands were shaking. A nervous film was swimming in her eyes. Without looking she sensed the bulk of the fat man rolling toward her in waves of sweat, till it covered the pimpled moon beside her. His hand fell heavily on her shoulder.

"It's all right Frank—it is Frank? Or is it Joe?—It's all right. She's with me."

"Still can't serve her without eye dee."

"Tell you what," the fat man said. "We'll have us a party. There ain't no law against a party, is there? You just set up two double bourbons, and two bottles of Coors, and have room service bring them to one-oh-nine." His stubby fingers tightened in her shoulder. "Me and Chicita here are gonna have us a party."

She wanted to push his fingers from her shoulder; but didn't want to touch his flesh. Instead she slipped off the far side of the stool, out from under his hand. His bulk was too flabby to react. She turned her back and moved away through the yellow-amber dark, clutching her wallet tight. The band had returned and was raising its instruments, brass throwing moonslivers at eye level now. Just before the first note sounded the fat man's epithet grabbed her from behind.

"Dumb Mex cunt!"

She didn't turn but hurried through the tables, out of the lounge and into the corridor. The fat man didn't follow. As if he would melt away in the light. Band music faded into the tinny Muzak of the lobby. Black glass doors ejected her into the night.

She found that she was sweating. A sky filled with stars mocked the city. Visions of fat men lurked on every corner. She thought of starting back toward the school. But couldn't. The walls of her room would close in, would choke her to death with inaction. She was forcing herself to be calm, to accept a Michaelless fate, but the platelets in her blood, childlike word she clung to from bio class, the platelets were marching, propelling her feet forward, deeper into the city. Propelling her toward some hazy resolution, some swift answering act of creation or despair.

A sign said Water Street. The dirty window of a hock shop was crowded with old pawn, and cheap carved figures of men and women. Treasures of dead Navajos being strangled by tourist junk. Up the block across the street a lean dog leaped across a sign. The bus station, where less than a year ago she had seen Robert leave.

She crossed, and peered through the door, thirsty and hesitant. A policeman was seated at the counter, sipping coffee, his dark blue hat beside his cup. A man with a blond crew-cut, wearing an army jacket, was jerking a pinball machine. The rest of the place was empty, except for a heavy, dark-haired woman behind the counter, a once-white apron covering mountainous breasts.

She pushed through the door, into a pinball ringing, and sat at the counter. Mountain woman in her dirty apron turned from a greasy grill she had been scraping.

"What would you like, dearie?"

"A Coke," she said.

The woman filled a wax-coated cardboard cup with crushed ice, and ran the Coke into the spaces between. When she placed the cup on the counter she spilled some. She wiped it, thick-fingered, with a rag smelling of floor mop.

The Coke tasted sweet and waxy, bubbles burning her throat. The pinball ringing had stopped, and she turned her head idly toward the games across the pale green terminal. The man with the blond crew-cut had stopped playing. He was in the middle of the room, and he was moving toward her, slowly, parting the air in front of him with his hands, as if her were pushing aside branches in a dense, dangerous forest. She looked at his face for a long second, remembering it from somewhere: pale blue eyes staring vacant out of young, gaunt features; very white. Quickly she turned back, and sipped at her Coke, and looked through the corner of her eye at the policeman, who was still sipping coffee at the far end of the counter.

She heard the young man's shuffling steps coming closer. Saw mountain woman puttering behind the counter, paying no attention. Sensed the young man standing slightly behind her. She held her breath. Waiting for something to happen. When nothing did, she turned. The young man's face was two feet from her own.

They stared at one another, with puzzled looks. She remembered. He was the same man who was playing pinball when she said goodbye to Robert, nine months before. He had banged the machine so hard he had bloodied his hand.

On his breast pocket was stenciled black lettering. It said: PUNZLE.

The man kept staring into her face. His eyes began to widen. Without warning, he screamed; driving her chest into a pounding. A wild, unintelligible scream. She jerked her head back, but the man was moving away, running across the station. He left his feet as he neared the far side, diving across the worn linoleum, head-first, like a baseball player. He slid on his chest among the legs of the pinball machines, wrapping his arms around his head. When he came to a stop, huddled in a corner, his red-faced shrieks came clearer.

"Gooks! The Gooks are here! Run for your lives! She's gonna blow us up!"

She looked toward the policeman, who was looking from her to the screaming man and back again. The policeman shrugged at her, and turned back to his coffee.

She felt a weight on her hand. Mountain woman was petting her with a greasy paw. She turned, to pull her hand away. Mountain woman was smiling, kindly. Two of her front teeth were missing.

"Don't be frightened, he won't hurt you. He don't mean no harm."

She looked toward the pinball machines. The man had stopped screaming. He was on his hands and knees, peering at her with a frightened look from underneath.

"What's the matter with him?"

"Gooks! Run!" the man cried again.

"He was in the war," mountain woman said. "It did somethin' to his head."

The man remained on the floor under the machine, curled up like a dog. His arms were protecting his face.

"Does he scream all the time?" she said.

"Just once in a while," mountain woman said. "Mostly when one of you Indian ladies comes in. Must remind him of somethin'." She ran her dirty rag

131

along the counter. "Showed up about a year ago. Been hangin' out here ever since. Don't know where he comes from, don't know where he sleeps. Eats burgers 'n' plays pinball, all day, all night. Gets a guvmint check at the post office sometimes, for his head. Says he's waitin' for his discharge, to go home. Home from the war."

Coins clicked on the counter. The policeman was standing, putting on his hat. She pulled out her wallet, unbottoned the change purse, put down money for the Coke. She didn't want to be there alone. She followed the policeman out the door.

"You okay?" the policeman said.

She nodded.

"You need a ride somewhere?" He had a slight Spanish accent.

"I can walk," she said.

The policeman shrugged. He circled into the street, and ducked into a blue patrol car parked at the curb.

She looked back through the glass door. Mountain woman was clearing the counter. The man hadn't moved from beneath the machines.

The lights of the patrol car flared, its engine hummed. Slowly she walked up the street. The patrol car pulled from the curb, and passed her, taillight winking red around the corner.

The streets were empty. At night the streets of Santa Fe were always empty. Store windows on the far side were lit by the full moon. On the near side she walked in shadow.

She thought of going back. She wanted company. Going back to mountain woman. To the man named Punzle. And his war.

She wasn't sure who had been the victim just now. Him, or her.

*****

She kept on walking. Despair settled over her again, like fog. The streets once more were mostly Michaelless. Behind each door was a pretty blonde woman, naked beneath an orange robe. She started to shake again.

She walked a narrow pavement, two feet wide, her shoulder brushing a windowless wall. She heard an ambulance racing, wailing at the moon. Racing out Cerrillos Road. She thought of the faceless driver in the car that had almost killed her. Wondered if, further out, he had wrapped his speeding car around a pole. Had cut his face. Had crushed his chest. Like her cousin Joe, who had gone riding in a pickup one day and never came back. A railroad train had smashed the pickup in half. One day they had seen him. The next day they would never see him again.

Like Michael.

She walked a wide pavement covered by a wooden portal. The pavement spilled her into a wide square, a block long, a block across. The Plaza. The center of town. Sunless now the curlicued white iron benches slept alone in the moonlight. Tall trees cast daytime shadows. Not a soul stirred. Not a dog, or a cat, or a cop. The stone obelisk stood alone in the center, erect and looming.

She was drawn to it. She walked to the center of the Plaza. Fingered the tips of the green-black iron fence that surrounded the monument. She read the inscription carved in the concrete base. "To the heroes who have fallen in the various battles with Indians." There was an uneven space before the word Indians, where a word had been chipped away. It used to say "Savage" Indians. Some people thought that was an insult. Not long before, a blond man, an Anglo, wearing a construction helmet, had come one morning with a hammer and a chisel and had chiseled the "savage" out. He disappeared before anyone knew what he had done. It was in the newspaper. Now there was no adjective. Blank Indians.

She sensed that someone was watching her. She turned. Across the street was the long facade of the Palace of the Governors. More than three centuries old, and still standing. No one was there. Unless he was skulking in the deep shadows under the portal, where the moonlight didn't reach.

Her eye fell on the clock on the far corner, standing tall in front of the museum; about fifteen feet high, four feet across the round face. She tried to see the time. Moonlight reflected off the staring glass. She walked to the side, beyond the angle of the glare. The black hands of the clock said 6:28. The clock had stopped. It must be about midnight, she imagined. She remembered seeing it in the paper. The clock didn't work. It was an old clock, and they had not gotten it to work since they had installed it the summer before. It stood now a monument of timelessness. Like the valley, where time came no closer than the white shining trails of the jets far above.

She turned her back to the clock. She felt again that someone was watching her. A large glass eye that didn't blink, didn't close. She felt faint. Her legs were leaden from walking. She sat on a white iron bench. And stared at another iron bench across the way. Michael was on it. She was on it. Michael was saying goodbye. Michael was afraid.

*****

She remembered when she had seen him for the first time: the morning after the pills. She went back further—to the night of the pills. She had stolen them from the room of a girl who needed them to sleep.

She remembered the terror of those nights in the early autumn. The lonely days of a new semester, no Robert to teach her, to comfort her. A dead baby left behind on the reservation, in the mouth of a grinning dog; its grave a dog's teeth, a dog's saliva. A dead father left behind on the reservation, dead naked in a sweathouse; dead drunk in a sweathouse. The hallways had echoed with the footsteps of Robert. She hadn't realized how she would miss him. How much she had leaned on him. She had other friends, but not real ones. None you could confide in. None you could tell of dead babies. She

134

hadn't even told her mother that. None you could tell of dead fathers. Not the truth of it. If it were possible to know the truth.

If she could have told her mother of the baby, she could have had the Evil Way sung over her, for the miscarriage. But she didn't tell her mother. The poisons remained inside her, all that summer. Poisons of the miscarriage, and some vague guilt she felt about her father, had always felt about her father, though she knew not why. Poisons from Santa Fe, from the white man's city. She had gone off to study, to paint. Had come home to a dead baby, a dead father. Nothing to show for her nine months except a roll of canvases and a feeling that somehow she had betrayed them all. The People didn't care about Success. They cared about the family, about the sheep. For centuries it had been their way. It had enabled them to survive. But she was smarter than that. She would go off, be a painter. Reach for higher values. Reach for Art. She had gone off, and had come home, but after the first few days, after the dead baby, the dead father, it hadn't felt like home any more. The outfit was friendly but somehow she felt apart. She had seen things they hadn't, and somehow the things they shared had become less important. Had melted away. She willed with all her might for it not to be so. But she couldn't will feelings; not theirs, not hers.

Uneasy in the valley for the first time in her life, seeing in the rock people only rocks, not people, she had returned for the new semester to the white man's world of Santa Fe, where she would have to live. And realized that she couldn't. Not without Robert to lean on. Robert or someone else. She had grown frightened, and listless. She had lost her will to paint. And without that, school was meaningless, the teachers were babbling fools, saying nothing. She began to cut classes, and lay on her narrow bed, staring up at the blank white of the ceiling. Wallowing in the martyrdom of irony. She had become a cliche. The Navajo who goes to the city, and can't survive, and goes back home, and has outgrown that. The Navajo of the sociologists, caught between two conflicting worlds. The Navajo of the cities; of Gallup;

of Page; of Holbrook. The drunken Navajo; except that she hated the taste of whiskey, couldn't drink more than a beer. A cliche, nonetheless.

She had seen what had happened, and felt she was stronger than that. She had reached deeper inside herself. Had traveled in her brain deep into the valley; had relived The People's past; had walked again with the sheep, in her mind's eye; had trafficked again with the rock people, people once more. Had seen bluebirds, rabbits, mice, eagles. Had returned to classes, had started painting again, more powerful than before. Had felt she had conquered cliches. That the future would take care of itself, if only she was strong. Had exulted in her strength. At her slim, shapely body in the mirror; had smiled at her own face in the midnight sky of hair. Nina Yazzie. Sweet Salt.

Then the nightmare had returned. Nightmare of the ghosts of dead Navajos. Striped through the door of dimless memory they crept; noiseless silhouettes, undulating purple fire; two shapes bound together, chains of rotting children round their necks; straining in dark to see their faces, blackness rising like tall police, blocking her view; kissing with blackened lips that weren't there, kissing harder, harder, on the lips; charcoal faces empty burned and hollow, coming closer, coming closer, laughing soundless laughs through silver teeth; holding a wolf before their eyes, wretched wolf grinding sharpened claws, clawing like a cat, coming for her eyes; eyes of glass that couldn't close; coming for her eyes...

She had cried out in her sleep, and lay awake, shuddering, on the narrow bed. Afraid to close her eyes. Afraid they would come again. Alone in the white man's city. The Singer had driven them away, two years before. They had followed her to the city.

Three nights they came. She lay awake, staring, and slept by day, sunlight warming in the window. Missing classes. Wondering. Her father was dead, had paid. What did they want with her? Dark circles spread beneath her eyes. Her belly hurt, from not eating. She thought of going back to the reservation. Did not want to go back. Not like this. Not in retreat.

The fourth night they came again. But with a difference. The blackness rising like tall police wasn't there, blocking her view. Green fire lit the awful dream. Nothing blocked her view. Striped through the door of dimless memory they crept; noiseless silhouettes, undulating purple fire; two shapes, bound together, chains of rotting children round their necks; green fire flickering in their faces, green fire lighting up their faces; faces no more buried in the blackness; faces coming closer. Faces not of Old Man Lives Alone, Old Woman Lives Alone, burned black in the fire, as she had thought. Faces much more familiar. Her own face. Her father's face. Kissing with blackened lips that weren't there. Kissing harder, harder, on the lips. She and her father, kissing, on the lips. Charcoal faces empty burned and hollow, holding a wolf before her eyes, coming for her eyes. Eyes of glass that couldn't close. Coming for her eyes. Chains of rotting children round their necks. She and her father. Kissing. On the lips. Laughing soundless laughs through silver teeth. She and her father. ..

Drowning in the dream she kicked and clawed her way to wakeful-ness. The room was spinning above her narrow bed. She fumbled for the light switch, turned it on; lay panting in the piercing light. Her pajamas were soaked under the armpits, clinging to her breasts. Taut nipples of her breasts. She shivered, and pulled the blanket to her chin. She stared into the white light of the bulb, blinded. Stared, blinded, till her eyes hurt with the pain of it. Forced herself to stare, unblinking. Forced herself to see, unblinking. Till her head hurt from the pain of it. Piercing points of pain, exploding lights inside. She shut her eyes. Purple shapes swarmed. Purple shapes of puzzles, falling into place. Purple shapes adding to the pain. Horrid letters danced on spinning prayersticks. Greek words with pointed elbows. Drooling refugees from psychology texts. Mute phrases from class the week before. Ancient myths, human skeletons, once bone, now stone, given eternal life by the printing press. By the written word. Embalmed myths picking at her brain. Unraveling her. Peeling away the layers of sanity. Shucking corn. Shouting

137

obscenities from sacred mountaintops. Shoving her face into excrement smells. Tying her down under pink layers of brain. Shouting. Her father's curse was not in his leg at all, but in his head! She twisted, in torment, on the bed. Pressed her nose deep into the pillow. Pulled the pillow ends around her ears. The shouting continued, unmuffled. Not wanting to hear. Hearing. Pulled the pillow tight across her eyes. Not wanting to see. Seeing. Saw her father in the dawn of her birth, staring at the dead wolf girl. Saw the future that he had seen in her face. A father's primal curse! Saw him fleeing, in terror, stepping in a hole, hurting his leg. Forcing the curse from his head into his leg. Escaping future sin with present pain. Pain that Hosteen Navajo couldn't kill. Because he treated the wrong place. She twisted and jerked on the bed, as if touched with cattle prods. Twisted the pillow in anguish, till it sent out a white feather, surrendering. Let the pillow fall, stared flatly, blankly, at the bulb. The light flared in bright white circles. Pain like a purple horse galloped into the past. Among the skeletons. Circled childhood scenes where he had kept away, because of the curse. An unfather. Crossed the teeming desert to Gallup, where he had gone to drink, after she had hugged him; after he had touched her cheek with flame. She twisted again, opened her eyes, to kill the purple horse. Before it could go further. The naked bulb glared, relentless. The horse galloped on. Carried her to the hogan of the old people, the day of the murders. She saw him raising his gun, pulling the trigger against their ancient moans, pushing their dying faces in the flames. On the day of her ceremony, the day she was ripe. Mere coincidence. Needing to kill the curse that day. Mere... She closed her eyes, fumbled for the switch, turned off the light. The light in her head remained. Lit a corral crowded not with sheep but with deer. The words that One Blue Eye had spoke about her father. He thought his sheep were deer, who could forage for themselves. She had foraged, but what of him? He was a deer owner. Like Deer Owner of the underworlds. She scratched at her eyes, pressed at her closed lids. The light wouldn't leave. Eyes that couldn't close. The story they

138

told of Deer Owner. He had his daughter for a wife! A story, a myth, nothing more. All people had them. Like what she was doing now. Imposing order where there was none. Imposing a pattern, when life had none. Confused by the books in school, psychology texts. Confused by her loneliness, her longing. He dared not touch his daughter, because the ghost was in him. Haunted by the sweathouse, his naked body inside. The bottles behind the door. Drinking again, because she was coming home. He should have known better. She saw him carrying logs from the woodpile near the hogan, building a fire outside the sweathouse. Heating the rocks till they were too hot to touch. Getting a shovel, scooping the hot rocks one by one onto the shovel, placing them carefully in the sweathouse.

"NO!"

She had cried out, sat up, in the emptiness of the room. Scratched at her eyes with her nails, drawing blood across her cheeks. Eyes she couldn't scratch away. Eyes that couldn't close. A question coming-toward her, like a ghost. A question she had never seen before.

Drunk, could he do all that?

Or had he prepared it before?

The only way he could find to kill the curse. . .

The only victory…

Trembling, she lay again in the darkness. Darkness of evil light. Feeling her bed a coffin. Waiting for it to close. Wishing she had been born dead. Then the others would have had a father. Her mother would have had a husband. If she had been born a boy. If she had been born dead. Tears ran from her eyes, across her temples, into her ears, as she lay exhausted and sweaty in the dark. In slow-motion films of black light the facts ran again and again through her brain. The arithmetic always the same. Her father's curse. Her.

*****

Dawn softened the window, gray and deathly. The world was a stench-filled pit, inducing nausea. A pit into which she would plummet, dizzily; spinning down and down, through endless caves of gray rock, into a bottomless whirlpool of gray water. Forever.

For three days she stood on the brink, looking down. Wandered aimlessly, a stranger in her own life. Walked into classes late, and walked out early, without a word; with no explanation to teachers or to class. Watched the whirling vortex of gray waters. Gave back her food to toilet bowls. White whirlpools of water. Mockeries. Wore sweaters in the heat. Went coatless in the cold. Oblivious. The campus a checkerboard square on a board that had no others, a board surrounded by white. No place to jump to. No place to move. Steep drop stretching below her, dizzily.

The third night a door was open down the hall. An invitation. An amber plastic bottle of pills standing on a dresser. Beckoning. She walked in, put them in her pocket, walked out. As simple as that. Went to her room, closed the door, but didn't lock it. So they wouldn't have to break it down. Nina Yazzie, thoughtful to the end.

She spilled the pills across her desk. Round and white, like aspirin. Pain killers. Monster slayers.

The only victory. . .

She went to the window. A pale sliver of moon was beyond the trees. She looked down, down into the street. Into the gray swirling. Felt her forehead touch the window. Felt that she was falling.

She stepped back. There was nothing she needed to do. No one here would care. She swept the pills off the desk into her hand. Some of them scattered, dancing, to the floor. She still held a handful. Quickly she stuffed them into her mouth. Swallowed some, choking, her cheeks full with the others. Stumbled to the sink and filled her glass with water, and swallowed the rest.

Nothing happened.

There was nothing more to do. She switched off the light. Pale yellow from the hall cracked under the door. She lay on the bed, face up, staring at the darkness. Waiting. Till her eyes grew heavy.

She dreamed of a knock on the door; of someone calling her to the telephone; of a counselor wanting to see her. She dreamed of a kitcarson stuffing a rifle down her throat.

*****

Alone on the Plaza in the night. Perspiration bathed her with the memory. She looked at the white iron bench across the way, where Michael had been. Michael who restored her to life. Whose caring had cleansed her of guilt. Whose listening had brought perspective. Whose logic had prevailed. Michael whose love had restored her innocence. Had given her rebirth. Michael who dared not touch her. Michael, who was afraid.

The white iron bench was empty. She was alone in the night.

A church bell tolled. A single bell, sounding pure. It was one o'clock in the dark.

The Cathedral of St. Francis was a block away. She was taken with a desire to see it. To follow that dark young Spanish archbishop who had smiled. To see what solace it could offer.

She walked across the Plaza, toward San Francisco Street. Stopped abruptly at the window of an art gallery that featured western paintings. Stared, shaken, at the single painting in the window: a large canvas of the valley, her valley, rock people pale and characterless in the distance. The window caught her own reflection, thin, transparent, in the center of the painting. Like the self-portrait she had done. Home Town Girl.

Hers was better.

She moved on, toward the robust cathedral looming square and solid in the dark. Up stone steps, past a bronze statue. Eager to see the religious

141

works inside, paintings of the past. Eager to make connections, ancient connections. Anybody's. To lose herself in the musk of darkened pews. To lament by candlelight. To purge by fire the ache of electric hearts. To gaze at Holy People. Anybody's. To reach out.

She pulled open a dark wooden door, and stepped inside. Disappointment cut her, instantly. The interior was large, and bright. Fluorescent bulbs bathed the beige ceiling. Microphones on steel rods split the pulpit, wires hanging down. Amplifiers stared brown from square posts. Pale blond pews, Danish modern. Wooden Jesus, carved yesterday. The whole place, somehow, a sham. A vast, false promise. An emptiness.

She let the door close behind her. Blasphemous. Wishing she had seen a priest eating a nun on the altar. Some sign of flesh. Some connection.

The street curved to the left. She followed adobe walls to a stretch of grass beside the Santa Fe River. More a wide, deep ditch than a river, though now, in April, it was gurgling with the spring runoff from the mountains. She peered over the edge. Moonlight filtering through trees that lined the bank had turned the ribbon of water to quicksilver.

A footpath wended through the grass beside the ditch. She followed it, idly, her legs moving toward some destination of their own. Further away from the school. Away from the loneliness that lay in waiting. As long as she walked there would be diversions: quicksilver ribbon, a bridge to cross it, old houses with split logs piled high on the porches. A glimpse of the black mountains, looming closer.

She turned on a street that rose gently toward the hills. Canyon Road. "The Arts and Crafts Road," a wooden sign said. Shops and studios of painters, potters, weavers, jewelers, glassblowers, leather-smiths, interspersed for two miles with adobe homes, cracked and crumbling but much sought-after. One of the oldest streets in the city, an Indian trail long before the Spanish arrived, narrow and winding, alive on spring afternoons with flaming yellow flowers as big as a man's skull, with old Spanish men in fedora hats leaning on ancient walls, and skinny dogs sleeping in the sun. But empty now; abandoned to the night. Dirt driveways running beside shops and houses to empty fields beyond.

A chill came over her, her sweater suddenly no protection from the night. She had walked too far. Her feet were leaden, would go no further. Moonlight cast strange shapes in unknown alleys, turning her head first this way, then that. She wanted to be away from this road, back at the dormitory, anyplace. And, turning, saw a pale light in a familiar shop up the street. The pottery shop of Michael's nice friend Buck. If he was awake she could rest for awhile. Perhaps he would drive her home.

She crossed the street, and peered in through the door. The front of the shop was dark, but a light was burning in the rear. She knocked on the door. Softly at first, then harder. The figure of Buck stood, a silhouette, and moved toward the front of the shop. He looked at her through the door, unlocked a latch, pulled the door open wide. A light flared over her head. Lighting his face.

*****

"We're here."

A hand was shaking her upper arm. Insistent. "We're here." Nina fought back from the memory. Opened her eyes. Her mother was looking at her. She couldn't remember where she was. The past was departing sluggishly. The present arriving even slower.

"Where? Where are we?"

"At the hospital?"

"The hospital?"

"In Tuba City."

143

A cramp gripped her belly, bringing her back with a jolt. Grim despair clamping across her temples. Her baby. Drying up inside. In the back of a truck.

The tailgate screeched down, her Uncle Tinker's face behind it. Lightpoints of sweat on his forehead. His voice sounding nervous.

"Can you walk?"

Nina pressed her hands against the cold bed of the truck, pushing herself upright; sitting. She tried to move her legs. They were numb from the ride. She shook her head.

"I'll get someone," Tinker said.

She watched the back of him crossing the pavement, moving through a gate in a cyclone fence, along a walk that split a grass lawn, through the glass doors of the building. The hospital looked modern, tan bricks, long and low; one story high, but still bigger than the one in Santa Fe. Street lights paled the stars. Beyond the hospital across the streets at either end were small private houses. Michael had lived in one of those. And worked in the hospital. And gone walking into the desert after work, feeling like an eagle.

And lost a wife.

"Does it hurt?" her mother said.

"A little. It comes and goes."

A cramp came again. She found the crumpled handkerchief tucked under the blanket, and squeezed it. Squeezed it into a ball in her fist. Tinker was walking quickly out of the hospital, followed by a man pushing a table that had wheels. Her mother pulled off the blanket. Nina pushed herself forward, to the back of the truck. Till her legs hung over the end. The man wheeled the table to the edge of the truck. Tinker stood beside her. She leaned forward, put her arms around his neck. "Easy now," he said. He put an arm around her waist, another under her knees, and lifted her from the truck onto the table.

"You can lie down," the man said.

144

The feeling had returned to her legs. "It's okay."

Her mother climbed down from the truck, and walked beside her, holding her hand, as the man pushed the table through the gate, up the walk to the hospital. Tinker held open the glass door.

"I'll go park the truck," he said.

The lobby was bright, with pale brown walls. She sat on the table as her mother talked to a nurse behind a desk, giving information the nurse was writing on a card. The man came back carrying a folded hospital gown, light gray, and put it on the table beside her. The nurse told him a room number and he pushed the table down the corridors, past doorways with slatted wooden doors, like saloons in western movies. Alongside each door were typed white cards with the names of people on them. Her mother walked alongside, looking nervously from door to door.

The man stopped the table outside a room, and went in and did something, and came out, leaving the doors open, and pushed the table in. Her mother followed. He helped her step down from the table and sit on the bed. The room was small. Across a space of six feet was another bed. The sheet was rumpled. Against the white pillow was the dark lined leather face of an old Navajo woman, her hair a streaky gray. Her eyes looking watery were gazing blankly at Nina. Her mouth hung open. Only one tooth was visible inside it. The tooth looked green. The woman disappeared as the orderly pulled shut the gray curtain that hung on a chrome bar above the bed.

The orderly mumbled something she didn't hear. Her mother nodded. The orderly left the room, closing the doors behind him. Her mother helped her pull the velveteen blouse over her head, and replace it with the hospital gown. She raised herself by pressing her hands on the bed, her elbows stiff. Her mother pulled off her skirt, and pulled the hospital gown over her pale moon belly.

There was a knock on the door. Without waiting for an answer another man entered. He was about Michael's age, with black hair, and a small black

145

beard pointed at the chin, and doctor's rubber wires in his breast pocket. He looked at a clipboard he was carrying, and said, "Mrs. Yazzie?" Her mother nodded. "I'm Dr. Brooks. And you're Nina?"

He turned back to her mother. "If you would wait in the waiting room down the hall, while we have a look."

Her mother squeezed her arm, and left the room. The doctor looked at his clipboard. As always with doctors her heartbeat was banging the drums of the Enemy Way.

"You've lost a lot of fluid?"

Nina nodded, nervous.

"Some blood, too?"

She reached out her hand, and gave him the handkerchief that was balled in her fist, soaked with perspiration now over the brown dry blood. He looked at it and put it aside.

"This is your first child?"

"Yes." Softly. Shyly.

"No other pregnancies? Miscarriages?"

Nina hesitated. "Last year, two months... I lost it."

The doctor took a pen from his pocket, and moved it toward the clipboard.

"Do you have to write that down?"

The doctor paused. "Why not?"

She felt her face flushing. She looked down at the floor. "Nobody knows. My family. . . "

The doctor put the pen away. He chucked her under the chin with the side of his fist. "It's our secret," he said.

He put the clipboard on the bed, and put his rubber wires in his ears. "Let's have a look. If you'll pull up the gown..."

Shyly, wriggling, she pulled the gown up over her waist.

"Higher," he said. "Just for a minute."

146

She held it under her armpits. The doctor listened through his wires to her heart; to her breathing. Then he leaned over further, and listened to her belly. To the baby. Quietly. Her breath coming quickly.

"This is your seventh month?" Still listening.

"Yes. The end of it."

"You're sure of that. It couldn't be earlier?"

Her face flushed again. "There was only one time."

The doctor stood, removing the wires from his ears. She let the gown drop over her belly.

"The baby . . .?"

"The baby sounds fine."

She smiled, with relief.

"If this were the fifth month, or even the sixth, you probably would have miscarried. The sac is broken, the fluid has drained out. A baby can't live too long like that. The body rejects it, like a foreign object. That's what your cramps are. The start of labor."

"But it's too soon," she said. Frightened again.

"Not in this case. The baby has to be born. In the seventh month, it can live in an incubator. Cozy as a mother's tummy. Assuming everything is all right."

She sat limp, the fear bubbling in her blood. Unable to think. The doctor continued talking.

"I'd like the baby to be born in the next few hours. To make sure nothing goes wrong inside. There are two things we can do. We can give you a drug, to induce labor. To see if you can have the baby naturally. I think that might work, since the cramps have started on their own. If not, if it doesn't work, we'll have to perform a Caesarian. Go in and get the baby. But we'll try the other first. Okay?"

Okay. What was there to say? She sat glumly, looking down. Heard a rustling in the sheet beyond the gray curtain. The lined old woman in the other bed. Wished she were alone. The doctor touched her chin again, lifting her face.

"Don't worry. It'll be okay." "You and the baby."

She tried to smile, but couldn't.

"I'll be right back," he said.

He left the room. Her mind was a blank white of nameless sorrow. Sadness of babies in small glass boxes with wires. Babies who would die. Wondered if the woman behind the curtain had any babies. Wondered what was wrong with her. She looked past ninety.

The doctor came back, carrying a long needle filled with fluid. "This should do the trick," he said. He pulled up the sleeve of her gown, dabbed alcohol on her upper arm. Jabbed the needle in. The skin popped and the needle drew a piercing deep line of pain. The doctor dabbed the spot again with alcohol.

"Why don't you lie down under the sheet now, and relax. Just let your muscles relax. Try not to worry. Think of something else. If you feel cramps, that's fine. Okay? I'll keep checking back, or I'll send a nurse."

She eased her legs up under the sheet, and lay back, slowly, to the pillow, her muscles tense. She pulled the sheet to her neck, her belly making a small white mound.

"Try to sleep if you can," the doctor said.

*****

She stared at the back of the doors. She heard the ancient woman behind the curtain breathing, unevenly. She stared, fuzzily, at the moon belly mound under the sheet. Stared into the mound as if it were a smokey crystal ball, the future obscure, only the past revealed. She saw again as through an evening fog the night of her long walk. The night her moon belly started to swell. Saw herself standing alone on Canyon Road, standing before the door of the

148

shop—-images fading, receding, coming back again—saw the silhouette of Buck moving from the rear to the front in answer to her knock, Michael's friend Buck who would drive her home, safe from the moonspooks of the night. Saw him peer at her through the door, and switch on a light above her head, a light that lit his face.

It wasn't Buck.

Her chest leaped in a quickened beat of fear.

"Is Buck here?"

"No."

"You're. . .Lupo?"

"Lobo. Do I know you?"

"Nina Yazzie. I was here a few times to see Buck. With Michael Kirschbaum."

"Oh yeah. Mike's chick. From the Indian school, right?"

His face was olive, with dark, wavy hair. His features looked flat, even in the light overhead; as if a strong palm had pushed them into his head. He was wearing blue jeans without a belt; and an undershirt. His shoulders were thick and muscular. Dark curly hair on his chest bunched at the scoop of the shirt.

"You want something? You want to come in?"

She was trembling, from cold and tiredness. And fear.

"I was out walking. I walked too far. I thought maybe Buck would drive me home."

"You shouldn't be walking alone this time of night. It's not safe."

"I know. I got frightened."

He took her hand. His was large and calloused. He smelled of leather.

"You're shaking." He pushed the door open wider. "You better come in and sit down. Warm up."

She stepped into the shop, dark except for the light coming from behind a partition in the rear. Wooden shelves to the right were lined with solid

149

moonshapes: pottery bowls, pottery pitchers, pottery mugs. Buck's work. Hanging from pegs on the opposite wall were leather jackets, leather vests, looking in the dim light like parts of people, and belts streaming down, like leather rain. Like whips. Lobo's work.

She followed him past a waist-high counter, past a work table beyond; through a doorway in the cardboard wall, to the lighted space. A small wooden table stood against the wall, chairs on two sides. Near it was a small refrigerator, with black chips in the enamel. Next to that an old two-burner stove. On a shelf above the table was a jar of instant coffee, and a pink box of sugar. She saw a cockroach scurrying across the shelf.

"Sit, relax," he said.

She sat. Through an open door to her left across the narrow space she saw a toilet bowl. Next to the door, steep narrow steps climbed through a hole in the ceiling.

He set a small glass in front of her, with ice cubes in it, and brown liquid.

"Drink that. It'll calm you down."

"What is it?"

"Bourbon."

"I don't think I like bourbon."

"Drink it, you'll feel better. It's all I have."

There was authority in his voice. It made her afraid. She had always been afraid of him. She didn't know why. She drank from the glass, hoping it would calm her fears. The bourbon burned her throat, burned her stomach. Warmed her. She drank again.

The old woman behind the curtain was choking. Rasping in a voiceless noise. Nina looked at the curtain. The noise stopped. The breathing resumed, more uneven than before. Nina's eyes fuzzy with the drug looked again at her belly. Vague cramps stirring inside. Looked at her belly, saw a table with bourbon. She tried to remember what they had said. What they had talked about. Could remember only finishing the bourbon, Lobo pouring another

150

with thick hands smelling of leather. Of animal hides. Feeling closer to her father for the drinking. Feeling warmness coursing through her, and talk of fish. Lobo saying when she had knocked he was about to feed his fish. Would she like to see his fish. Climbing the steep ladderlike stairs through the hole in the low ceiling, into a small room with another low ceiling. The flat of his palm pushing up her rear as he climbed behind her. To a gray room with a mattress on the floor, sheets and bedding tangled in a heap. And beside it on a table a large glass case filled with water, and fish swimming. An aquarium. Pebbles, snail shells, tiny green plants filled the bottom. Green and purple lights glowed inside. Two dozen fish swam back and forth, little gold fish, little black fish, little red fish; two-color fish, black and gold, black and red; darting and swimming, back and forth, back and forth. Lobo dumped powder from a small box into the water. The fish streaked toward the top, fighting for the food. Ravens devouring a carcass.

"That's Gail," Lobo said, pointing to one of the fish. "That one is Nancy. That's Marilyn. That's Margaret. That's Betsy. That one there is Linda."

"They're all lady fish?"

"They all have girls' names."

He drew her closer to the tank. He pointed to two small fish in a space closed off from the rest.

"You see those two?"

She leaned over the tank. Feeling light-headed from the whiskey.

"Those were born yesterday. They don't have names yet."

She heard someone speaking A voice she barely recognized as her own. A voice drifting through a thick morning fog, or a storm cloud laden with dust. A voice her own and yet outside herself, the way it sounded on the tape recorder at school. As if it were coming from far away, as far away as the valley, carried by the wind.

"Maybe one of them is Nina."

He straightened up. Put his hands smelling of leather on her shoulders. A smile creasing his face like a scar.

"I was thinking the same thing."

He leaned forward, and kissed her. Pressed thick lips smelling of whiskey into hers. Pressed his chest into hers. Pressed his tongue into her mouth. She didn't like him. She let him. Let him remove her sweater. Let him open the buttons of her blouse. Let him press his large mouth to her breasts, licking sucking. Let him open her belt, let him pull her jeans and underwear down over her hips, let him press his face into her thighs, flat face seeking her, finding her. Watched the top of his head, the black hair, like some animal, sniffing, gnawing.

He pulled back, stood, pulled his undershirt over his head, catching it on his ears. She half sat, half fell to the mattress on the floor; and took off her sneakers; and pulled off the jeans that were bunched below her knees. Listening to him talk as he stood above her, undressing.

"You ever get licked off by a dog? One of them Indian dogs, out there in the desert? I guess it's different with a chick. You'd have to train him. I had this dog, an Irish setter. Really should name one of the fish after her. Big Molly. I used to smear some gravy on me, and let her lick it off. Fantastic. She died in the saddle, Big Molly. Just like John Garfield."

He had taken off his shoes, was standing on one leg, pulling off his jeans. His tight white shorts looked gray.

"It was a hot day in the summer, right after closing. I was working on some leather, wearing just Bermuda shorts. All of a sudden I got turned on. Really got the urge. I had some gravy in the fridge. I pulled off my pants, and lay down on the floor, right behind the counter, and smeared the gravy on, and let Molly do her stuff. She had this great, long think pink tongue. Fantastic. She was workin' and workin', gettin' every last drop of gravy, licking me big and red as a baseball bat. I'm lyin' there goin' crazy. Two, three more licks and I'm ready to pop. Suddenly a dog starts barkin' outside. I

152

thought the door was locked, but I had forgot, and left it open. Molly hears the barkin', and takes off, across the shop, and out the door, which had blown open. I'm lyin' there behind the counter, big as the Washington Monument, ready to pop, figuring she'll come back in a second, for more gravy. A minute passes, and finally I hear her comin'. Only it's not the dog. It's a lady's voice up by the counter, saying, 'Is anybody here?' I don't know what to do. If she walks past the counter toward the back, she'll see me lying there. So I figure, if I stand up, she can only see to my waist. I'll get rid of her. I'll tell her we're closed. So I stand up, to see this biddy, and it ain't no biddy, it's this gorgeous blonde chick, wearing a sleeveless yellow top, with tits out to here, and brown nipples big as silver dollars showing through. 'I'm sorry, we're closed,' I say. It kills me to say it. I want to come on to her. But there I am, behind the counter, getting closer to popping every second, and I can't take my eyes off them great brown nipples. Go 'way, go 'way, I'm thinking, but she stands there and says. 'Do you have an Irish setter?' I tell her I do, standing there dying, wanting her to get the hell out. Wanting to throw her on the floor and slam it to her right there. Wondering what the hell she's talking about. And she says: 'I'm sorry. It dashed out right in front of the car. I hit the brake, but it was too late. It wasn't my fault, really. It's lying out there, bleeding. You better come.' You better come, she says. I'm standing there like a dummy, naked behind the counter, almost startin' to drip, and she's standing there with the greatest tits I ever saw, waitin' for me to come get my dying dog."

He was naked, excited by his own story. She felt revolted, sickened. He was despicable, worse than she had imagined. She didn't want to hear any more, wanted to be away from there, anywhere; but it was too late. There was no way she could leave, not now. No place to run to. No place to hide. She told herself he had made it up, a story he used to arouse himself, to arouse his other girls. His other fish. She would stop listening, would get it over with, as quick as possible. Would submit. Would think of something

153

else. Of someone else. She stretched herself wide on the mattress, flat on her back, eyes closed, legs spread, arms pinned wide to the side. Imagined shackles of iron around her ankles, around her wrists, pinning her wide and open, spread-eagled on the sand. The way they raped Indian girls in the movies. Felt her back itch on the dirty sheet. Imagined yellow roaches running below.

"You're beautiful."

His voice was breathless with admiration. Of mooncolor curves and mounds of flesh, and tufts of hair. Of a feast that lay spread before him. Her.

She left him sinking to his knees on the mattress, moving up between her legs, pinioned but not pinioned, his story left hanging at the wide open sight of her. Saw Mexican bandits galloping on horseback, raiding the weary Indians on the Long Walk, stealing the wife of Many Horses, the wife Smiling Woman, throwing her baby off a cliff, taking her away. Saw blonde women in yellow sleeveless tops, naked under orange robes. Saw Graydog, chopped and bleeding in the snow. Blackened faces in a smokey hogan. A dead girl lying on a sheepskin, lined old people looking down at her. Smelled leather, smelled animal hide, and felt him hovering above her, breathing heavily, his thickness sniffing at her warm. Seeking entry.

She opened her eyes, to watch his face at the moment. His face was close, fuzzy. Above his shoulder on the low ceiling she saw something dark and looming. A poster, with a picture on it, large, lifesize, the picture of a large gray dog, its teeth bared, leaping toward her, lit by the green and purple of the fish tank. Leaping toward her, setting off small silent screams inside.

"What's that?" she said. "On the ceiling?"

He grunted, still seeking entry. Feeling her tighten.

"A poster. From the university. Your friend Michael gave it to me."

He pushed harder, trying to get in.

"A dog?"

"No, my nickname. A lobo. A wolf."

154

She screamed. Screamed as loud as she could. Tried to get up, scratching at his back. He slapped her face.

"What the hell's the matter?"

She screamed again. He shut it off by forcing his mouth against hers, forcing his tongue inside her, his mouth inside her. She ripped his back with her nails, drawing blood, fighting, clawing. She tried to close her legs. His knees were positioned between. She raised her legs, pounded his back with her heels, as hard as she could. Excited, wild, he drove in, into her warm, penetrating deep. Her legs were around his back, kicking, pounding; then losing strength, from her long walk. Steep descent into a lower world. Of monsters not yet slain. Squeezing, squeezing hard, his hairy, sweating body in between. Weary legs wilting. As if at last they had reached a destination. Had satisfied a primal curse. Had completed a long circle, of life, and death, and life again.

As is the natural order.

She twisted her head to the side. Wrenched her mouth from his. Went limp. A princess in a movie. Sweet Salt. Home town girl. Her eyes fell on the fish tank above, glowing green and purple. Saw the dark shapes of fish, swimming, back and forth, back and forth, back and forth, back and forth. Eyes wide open, avoiding the ceiling, concentrating with all her strength on the fish. Back and forth. Back and forth. Faster. Faster.

Till the were-wolf shuddered. And died.

*****

Hands were lifting her. Light. Dark. Light. Dark. Light. Dark. Lights rolling on the ceiling. She gripped her belly, bloated, covered with a sheet. Felt herself hurtling on the table with wheels, down a corridor with lights overhead. Light, dark, light, dark, through wide doors, into another room. Light. Darkened by faces, dark hair, pointy beard. The doctor.

"Where am I?"

"In the delivery room. You're going to have your baby."

Baby of swimming fish. Back, forth, back, forth. Baby born too soon, baby born too small. Baby they will put in a glass case. An aquarium.

"Doctor?"

"Yes?"

"If anything happens to me, will you see about the name?"

"Don't worry, you'll be fine."

"I don't know. . . I feel strange. . . If anything happens to me...if it's a boy. . . his name is Michael Kirschbaum. Michael Kirschbaum Yazzie."

"Mike Kirschbaum? The doctor who used to work here?"

His face was growing fuzzy, drifting out of focus.

"Michael K. Yazzie.. .Cherry Tree... Michael Cherry Tree."

A great wave of pain swept across her belly, like a sand dune drifting. Pain not in one spot but washing like fire across the whole lower half of her. Pain subsiding, leaving her gasping, reeling, then coming again, inexorable, like the future. Her eyes focused on the beard, doctor's black triangle of hair. The beard, outside of her, that was causing the pain. Her eyes fled to the ceiling, to a round white glass light, light that was causing the pain. Pain in still another racking wave. Closed eyes saw hogans of the past, strewn with weeds and ghosts. Hogans projecting pain into her belly. Underground houses of the dead. Snakes and white-skinned dogs. Emitting signals into medicine-smelling air. Triggering flowered trumpet-wails of pain, piercing all the darkened rooms. Pain swinging through her like a tractor-trailer truck; like shovelfuls of sand hitting a coffin. Quiet spaces between, allowing her to relax her fingers that hurt from squeezing the tablesides near her hips. Then rolling in again, thick black thunderclouds, rolling, spitting, splashing, amber waves of pain. Splashing beads of sweat onto her forehead, under her arms; onto her scalp beneath the midnight sky; in all the hairy places.

156

Cool air was bouncing off the sweat. Hands were pulling her arms, lifting her, so she sat. The gown fell to her waist. Not the gown, it wasn't there anymore, but a sheet. Somewhere she had been stripped. The sheet folding in her waist freed her breasts, sweating underneath. The doctor holding a needle was touching the curve of her back. His voice enlarged in a deep canyon hollow.

"This will stop the pain. The baby is coming."

A knife jabbed deep into her lower back. Into her spine. She was being murdered, silently. Cut in half, like a rotting tree. They laid her down again. A sprint of death, an absence, chased the pain across her belly, a dog chasing a cat across a clearing; till both were out of sight, and only peace remained.

They pushed her knees up toward her chest, blocking her view. The sheet thrown to the floor. They were working between her thighs, doctor's hands, nurse's hands. She looked at the mirror on the ceiling. Her moon belly glowing. Her nether hair glistening, like a crow. Hands darting about like naked birds. A knife slicing her, feeling nothing, a thin ribbon of red in the mirror. Hands reaching in, into the enlarged wet underside of her, as into the bowels of the earth; into the reed-hole where the Holy People came. Where life began. And sometimes death. Into the wet spongy flesh, twisting; pulling; grabbing hold. Pulling her inside-out. Like a used-up sock, smelling. Pulling her inside-out through a hole in herself. Pulling it free, cutting dangling cords, spaghetti hanging loose, messily. Slapping the pulpy mess, for some forgotten original sin. Making it cry. Making music.

They held it in front of her, boiled, red. Large testicles dangling. They laid it on her belly, its head between her breasts. Boiled red pinched moon, between the round chocolate nipples it would suck. Her muscles melting with the delicate sweetness of summer.

She cupped her hand on its boiled bottom, lest it fall. The nurse was working at the fork of her legs, where they would sew.

"Doctor!"

There was impatience in the nurse's voice. And alarm.

"Doctor Brooks!"

The bearded face came closer, and frowned between her knees. The nurse moved around, tried to take her baby. She cupped its bottom tighter, not letting go. The nurse with strong hands bent her fingers, and pried the baby away. She tried to say no, to protest, but no words came. She had no strength to speak. On all sides there was new activity, strange faces over white coats, circling, as if she had become the eye of a storm. Her eyes, darting desperately, found the mirror overhead. Found her pale moon belly, and the dark crow beneath. The crow was dying, of a broken neck. Blood was pouring from its mouth. A thick red river, spreading into an ugly red lake, in the mirror, on the table, between her legs.

Faintness shrouded her eyes with a gauze curtain. Muffled orders barked in white masks. A cord tightened on her arm. She wanted to be afraid; and didn't have the strength. A black rubber mask descended from the sky; coming toward her eyes; blacking out her face. Kitcarsons stuffing rifles down her throat. Till there was only dark. Darkness and peace.

*****

Land of the anesthetic. Land without memory. Caves within catacombs. Pools of water dripping into a void. A black car drove lightless on a black road in the black night. Bears did tricks for painted clowns on TV sets with plugs pulled out. The universe at a long table ate mousefeet soup. Babies' heads peeped blonde and curly from the stiff crotches of trees. The snow fell red. Nina took black pills, and didn't remember. Darkness and peace.

*****

She awoke in the recovery room. Was pushed through light and dark, through wooden doors. The pale gray curtain hung in folds against the wall. The other bed was empty. It was turned down neatly, with fresh linen. The old woman was gone. If there had really been an old woman.

They lifted her onto her bed. They gave her small white pills, and water in a paper cup. Water trickled down her chin. She slept.

*****

The wind, pregnant with dust, swirled in a thick brown curtain across the mesa. It snatched up tumbleweed, and rolled it across the sand, like invisible children rolling hoops, or rubber tires. It shivered the branches of trees, forcing them to sing; or weep. A mad musician, playing mournful tunes. Surfaces were lost behind the thick brown curtain. Only shapes remained.

Weary of its burden, the wind dipped into the valley, to rest. Sand whirled in a canyon hollow halfway up a cliff. Sand scraped the concave wall of the hollow, the rocks alive with childish drawings; faded, but not invisible.

A woman sat in the hollow, a blanket on her shoulders, a child in her arms, watching a faraway eagle crossing the white trail of a jet; till jet and eagle together dissolved in the sand.

The woman looked at the sheep grazing below. They did not seem bothered by the wind. From above they looked like a stolid gray river flowing across the land; flowing from the past, into the future. A river temporarily in her care.

To the sheep, she was a god.

www.ingramcontent.com/pod-product-compliance
Lightning Source LLC
Chambersburg PA
CBHW050751250626
47155CB00005B/2012